KEITH ADAMSON is a retired architectural technician, living with his partner in south-west Spain after having worked for over fifty years in the construction industry in Glasgow. An appreciation of Mackintosh is in the blood of anyone associated with architecture in Scotland, and Adamson considers himself no exception. Writing has always been his main other sphere of interest and this is how he continues to spend his days, having a number of unpublished novels on his hard drive. In the 1980s and '90s he had some success with a few short stories included in various anthologies such as *Oranges and Lemons, The Freezer Counter* and *Borderline, the Mainstream Book of Scottish Gay Writing*. This is his first published novel.

C000163193

My Margaret,
Your Toshie

KEITH ADAMSON

Luath Press Limited

EDINBURGH

www.luath.co.uk

First published 2023

ISBN: 978-1-910022-81-8

Passages on pp 106–71 are freely adapted by the author from Charles
Rennie Mackintosh's letters to Margaret Macdonald Mackintosh,
as published in Pamela Robertson (ed), *The Chronycle: The Letters
of Charles Rennie Mackintosh to Margaret Macdonald Mackintosh*,
1927 (2001), © Hunterian Art Gallery, University of Glasgow.

Printed and bound by Severnprint, Gloucester

Typeset in 10.5 point Sabon by Lapiz

PART I

CHAPTER I

LIKE ANY TEN-YEAR-OLD boy, Billy English had little sense of the passing of time. When he wandered along the fore-shore at Walberswick-on-Blyth, engrossed in beachcombing, or simply letting his attention be caught by an oystercatcher that had been keeping just a matter of yards away from him, he hardly noticed how close the sun was to the horizon or how soon it would be dark. Only too well aware of her son's failing in this respect, Martha resigned herself to trusting that his stomach wouldn't fail to bring him home – indeed, he would probably catch the scent of her boiling pot of mutton, and follow it back to the kitchen as unerringly as a foxhound on the trail of its quarry.

Nevertheless, the sound of the latch on the kitchen door made her heart jump with relief, and she tried to feign non-chalance as she asked, 'So, where have you been to this hour?'

She already knew the answer, because it was always the same: 'Oh, just walking. Hunting for whelks.' Billy took off his jacket and threw it over the back of a chair. 'I saw a star-fish in one of the rock pools.'

'Did you, now?' Despite herself, Martha always found herself drawn into her son's account of his day.

'There were two herring gulls fighting on one of the breakwaters. One of them might have taken some scraps out of a bin.'

Billy made a bid to help himself to one of the potatoes draining in the colander, but his mother slapped the back of his hand.

'That man was there again,' he said. 'Near the ferry.'

That wasn't something she wanted to hear, and a little knot of anxiety returned to her throat. 'What man?'

7

'You know, the man with the cloak and the funny hat.'

She remembered Tom having said that the newcomer, with his deerstalker hat and pipe, bore a resemblance to Sherlock Holmes.

'What was he doing?'

'Nothing much. He went limping down to the shore and got so near the water I'll bet he got his boots wet. Then he just stood and looked out to sea. I watched him for a bit, but I got bored after a while and it was getting dark, so I thought I'd better get back along the beach.'

He made a second attempt to steal a small potato, this time with success, and continued his story with his mouth full. 'Later on, after I got back to the green, when I came around the corner, he suddenly turned up right in front of me. The moon was up by that time, but I still never saw him until he was almost on top of me. He made me jump good and proper.'

'Did he speak to you?'

'Yes, he said, "Did you enjoy your walk?" He speaks funny. Like a foreigner.'

'And what did you say?'

'I said I had enjoyed it very much, thank you, sir.'

'And then...?'

'And then I came home.'

Martha could tell there was nothing more to be gleaned from Billy about the man with the club foot. She told him to go and wash his hands for supper, before hauling the mutton bone out of the pot on the stove and placing it on the board so she could attack it with her cleaver. The stranger had been the subject of speculation between her and her husband, not to mention others in the village, for several months now, and Tom was a little wary of him. The couple had come down from Scotland last year, a matter of weeks before the war with Germany was announced, and were renting rooms in

Westwood Cottage. It was Mr Mackintosh's habit to walk down to the Anchor Inn of an evening and take a drink or two. Sometimes he went to the Bell Hotel, or to both, one after the other. But he always sat on his own and never spoke to anyone except the landlord.

When Tom got home, the girls came through to the kitchen and the family took their places around the table.

'You might not get any more meat after this,' said Martha. 'It's getting increasingly difficult to come by. Mr Round kept this joint by for me, but he warned me it could be the last one.'

'Then we'll just have to eat beans,' said Esther, and Billy blew a raspberry.

'That's enough, Billy,' said Tom.

'Dad,' asked Billy, 'why do we have to keep the blinds down now?'

'It's the blackout,' said Tom. 'If the Germans come over, they'll look out for lights on the ground to target their bombs.'

Martha gave Tom a look and shook her head. She didn't like such talk in front of the children.

'They better not drop any bombs on us,' said Billy.

'Billy bumped into the Scotsman again today,' said Martha, changing the subject. 'He asked Billy if he'd enjoyed his walk.'

Tom raised his eyebrows. 'Perhaps you should stay away from him.'

'I don't see why. He's okay. He gave me half of one of his sandwiches. And he's a good drawer. He showed me how to draw a daisy.'

'He showed me how to draw a daisy!' said Esther, mimicking her brother. 'Is that what you want to do? Draw daisies?'

'He draws buildings too. He showed me a drawing he's made of the smoke shed.'

Tom smirked. 'He could get into trouble drawing that. It's not just a smoke shed.'

The children looked at him quizzically.

'What is it, then?' asked Martha.

But Tom just tapped the side of his nose.

* * *

The English family weren't the only ones wondering about the strange Scotsman. Almost everyone in the village was anxious to know what his business was and the Cooper girl, who was a scullery maid at The Towers, just along from Westwood Cottage, was a rich source of gossip.

'That man,' she said to Martha, while she was queuing in the butcher's shop, 'the one staying in the cottage. He's supposed to be Scotch, but he doesn't sound like any Scotch person I've ever heard. None of the herring girls down at the harbour speak like him.'

'So, what do you reckon, then, Doris? Where do you think he's from?'

'Well, of course I don't really know, but it could be that he's just covering up his real accent. Which just might be...' she lowered her voice. 'Maybe he's German.'

Martha was horrified. 'What about his wife? Is she a German too?'

Doris put her finger to her lips and glanced quickly about her before replying. 'Could be... I don't know. But I know this. She's gone off up to Glasgow and left her husband to fend for himself. I know because Mrs Barnet told me, and her husband has the keys to the cottage.'

'That's strange.'

'And on Tuesday night I saw this lamp flashing in the upstairs window. Like maybe he was signalling to somebody out at sea.'

By now, Martha was convinced that all was not well and whispered conspiratorially.

'Perhaps we should tell somebody.'

Doris nodded. 'I think we should. Somebody in authority.'

*   *   *

As Margaret Mackintosh came within sight of Westwood Cottage after trudging the two miles from the station, she was puzzled to see the house in darkness. Letting herself into the parlour, she found the room in a state of disarray, as if it had been broken into. Every cupboard door was open, and drawers were pulled out with their contents all over the floor. One of the chairs was tipped over on its back and the standard lamp was leaning at an angle against the wall. There was no sign of her husband.

At The Bell, everyone looked up as Margaret walked in. She didn't usually grace the bar with her presence, and the sudden appearance of this statuesque lady with luxuriant red hair and calm grey eyes, daring to enter such an establishment unaccompanied, commanded the attention of both clientele and staff.

'Has anyone seen Mr Mackintosh? Has he been in here this evening?' she asked, addressing nobody in particular and trying to disguise the rising panic in her voice.

The barman put down the glass that he had been wiping, beckoned to her and leaned over the counter, speaking quietly.

'Mrs Mackintosh, your husband has been taken to the police station in Southwold. I think you should go there right away.'

'Is he all right?'

'That's all I know, I'm afraid.'

Margaret looked around, wondering if anyone could drive her there, failing which she'd have to persuade the ferryman to take her across the River Blyth. Tom English had been watching her since she came in, and now caught her eye. He knocked back his drink and came over to the bar.

'I need to go into Southwold, Mrs Mackintosh. Why don't you come with me?'

Grateful for the offer, she suspected that Tom was simply being kind; but it had been a long and tiring journey from Glasgow down to London, and then the little train to Walberswick seemed to take an age. The thought of a further two-mile walk into the town was almost too much to bear.

'Thank you so much,' she said. 'I don't suppose you have any idea what's happened? The cottage looks as though it's been ransacked.'

'I'm sorry, I don't know any more than you do. I'm sure there's just been some sort of mix-up.'

Margaret shook her head, imagining that her husband had somehow got himself into a drunken brawl, although that wouldn't account for the state of the cottage. While she waited for Tom to fetch his trap, all sorts of scenarios flitted through her mind.

* * *

'Yes,' said the sergeant at the desk. 'We have your husband in the cell. He was arrested by the military this afternoon. There are some questions about security.'

'Security?' Margaret couldn't understand what he was talking about. 'Of the cottage?'

'Of the nation, Mrs Mackintosh.'

Suddenly the reason for the cottage being in such a state became clear. 'What on earth did they think…?'

'You'd have to ask them, Mrs Mackintosh.' He handed her a card bearing the name of a captain in the Royal Navy.

'Can I see my husband?'

A visitor in the cell wouldn't altogether comply with protocol, but there was something about the lady's manner and bearing that made it impossible to deny her request.

The sergeant led Margaret to the block at the rear of the police station, opened the cell door and waited outside. 'You have ten minutes,' he announced.

Charles was in a state of high agitation. 'Well, am I glad to see you. For God's sake, tell these stupid buggers that they're mistaken.'

Margaret put her hand on his arm and gave him a light kiss on the cheek. 'Toshie, you have to keep your temper. Language won't help.'

'I suppose. Tell me about your trip. How was your sister?'

'Oh... the usual.' Margaret ran her hand through her hair. 'Frances won't listen to reason as far as Bertie's concerned. I told her we all love Bertie, but.... Well, it didn't do any good. She still dotes on him, of course.'

She sat down on the hard bench that would serve as a bed. 'We'll talk about that later. Tell me how on earth you ended up in here.'

'It was a raid. Twelve bloody soldiers with bayonets, for God's sake. They thought I was using the oil lamp to signal to the Hun. Can you imagine? I was only trying to light the bloody thing.'

'But you told them...?'

'Of course I told them. They wouldn't listen to anything I said.'

'I hope you kept your temper.'

'No, I bloody well did not. They had no business being there. No right to search through my stuff as if I were some common criminal. They ended up having to restrain me physically.'

Margaret's heart sank. 'Well, that wouldn't have helped. What were they looking for?'

'Evidence that I was a spy, apparently. Of course, they found the letters from Hoffman and the ones from Olbrich and Hermann Muthesius. I saw the officer pick them up, and when I tried to grab them out of his hand, they fell on the floor, and then everyone could see they were in German. Can you imagine? They seem to think they contain some sort of code.'

Margaret could imagine only too well. If they thought he was signalling to the Germans out at sea, and then came across all that correspondence from Germany and Austria, it was hardly looking good.

'Oh, and the sketch I did of the smoke house. They took that. "You have no business making drawings of the harbour," they said. Obviously, the smoke house is the nerve centre of the War Office.'

Margaret began to see the funny side and a barely suppressed smile flickered across her face.

'It's not funny. Tell them I'm a famous architect and they have to let me go.'

She took his hand. 'You're going to have to stay here tonight. I'll wire Patrick Geddes in the morning and see if he can help.' Patrick had been a good friend to them both while he had been living in Edinburgh, and had earned himself a number of influential acquaintances during his time in London.

In bad grace, Charles accepted her word for it.

*   *   *

In the morning, Charles was taken to the town hall and questioned by a magistrate and the captain of a Royal Navy ship that was anchored out in the bay. Margaret had walked over from Walberswick and provided the court with her and her husband's personal details. She had to spell her own name,

Margaret Mempes Macdonald Mackintosh, three times before they got it right. Her husband took the view that the whole affair was beneath contempt and refused to say anything. The officials were clearly running out of patience, although they were inclined to heed Margaret, whose manner was that of a lady of a substance and somebody to be reckoned with.

'These letters,' she said, 'are mostly personal correspondence. Charles is an artist and has a publisher in Berlin. If it hadn't been for the war, we were planning to visit Paris, Berlin and Vienna.' They were clearly sceptical. 'I can read German,' she offered. 'If it helps, I could translate them for you.'

'My dear lady,' sighed the magistrate, 'we can hardly take your word for the content of these letters. We would have to get them translated by a disinterested third party. Somebody from Cambridge.'

'And in the meantime...?'

'In the meantime, we'll hold on to them. The best we can offer you now is that your husband be subject to house arrest in Walberswick. We'll keep his passport until the situation is resolved.'

* * *

When they returned to the cottage, Charles looked disconsolately at the mess, but made no attempt to pick anything up. He walked over to the window and stared out across the sea.

'Can you imagine? Me. A spy?'

'How supercilious they were,' said Margaret. 'Self-important, pumped-up petty officials.'

'That magistrate kept calling me "Mr Rennie-Mackintosh" as if I were some double-barrelled aristocrat.'

'Mr and Mrs Rennie-Mackintosh,' said Margaret in a high voice, imitating the announcement of a footman at a society dinner, 'from Walberswick.'

Charles began to laugh. 'The Rennie-Mackintoshes fae Glesca,' he corrected, and for no apparent reason, their laughter rose to near hysteria as a relief from the nightmare of the last two days.

The next day, Margaret received a call from Anna Geddes. Her husband was heavily engaged in checking the proofs of his latest book, but of course he would pull whatever strings were necessary to get Toshie off the hook. She added that Patrick had insisted the Mackintoshes come to stay with them in London, for clearly they would no longer be welcome in Walberswick.

'It's going to be like being cast out of paradise,' said Charles. 'I'm not sure if London's the answer.'

Margaret could see only too well that this was the case. Toshie loved it here, and he had been productive with his watercolours, some of which she'd been able to sell. Admittedly, she'd had to approach his old client, Mr Davidson, but he was of a generous nature and had said he'd be delighted to buy one of Toshie's paintings. How were they going to live in London, so far from the natural surroundings that Charles craved, and with the ever-present threat of air-raids?

'I'm sure we'll manage,' she said.

'I'm sure we shall,' said Charles. 'But it won't be like the old days.'

CHAPTER 2

'OF COURSE, IT can never be like the old days,' said Margaret, as Meg Morris served her tea in the first-floor sitting-room of her home in Cheyne Walk. 'Those days are long gone.'

The Geddesses had made them feel very welcome, and after staying with them for a few days, Margaret and Charles developed a liking for the area and thought they should find a place of their own. Margaret began investigating some properties and soon found them a house to rent in Chelsea with a studio that met both their artistic requirements, and before long they had sought out a social scene of like-minded people: a collection of artists and writers that felt like their natural milieu. The group met informally at the Blue Cockatoo, a restaurant owned and run by a formidable lady with a bouffant hairstyle, by the name of Hettie Swaisland, and it was there that Charles and Margaret were able to renew their acquaintance with the painter John Duncan Fergusson, whom they had met on a few brief occasions in Glasgow shortly after they were married. Fergusson was now living in London with his partner Margaret Morris, with whom he had fallen in love while studying painting in Paris. She was an accomplished and innovative dancer, seventeen years his junior, but their attraction to each other had been instant. The couple, who preferred to be known as Fergus and Meg, had spent a year in France together before heading back to Britain and taking up residence in Chelsea.

'What about the old days?' asked Meg, offering Margaret another scone, which she politely declined. 'How did you and Toshie meet?'

Margaret sipped her tea. 'Well, my life changed when I was eighteen and my father decided to up sticks and move the whole family back to Glasgow. I suppose he had always been a little homesick for Scotland. He installed my brother Charles as a clerk in my uncle's firm of solicitors, in which he himself had been a partner before he and my mother moved to Tipton. Frances and I had both been at art college in Stoke, and would have been quite content to stay there. But you know how it is – when you're young, you think your father knows everything, and when he said we'd do better in Glasgow, we thought he must be right.'

'And was he?'

'Yes, as it turned out. In more ways than one. He wasted no time enrolling us in the Glasgow School of Art, and we both soon found our feet. That was where it all started. I can't remember exactly when we met Toshie and Bertie, but we had that instant connection... you know, as if we had always been friends. So, we became known as "The Four": Toshie, Bertie, Frances and me, and we were the first of "The Immortals".' She laughed at the thought of it. 'Sounds a bit ironic now, doesn't it?'

'"The Immortals?"'

'That was the name we adopted for our study group. Really, it was all John Keppie's doing.'

'Toshie's boss?'

'Yes. He used to invite us and some of the other students down at weekends to stay in a pair of bungalows that he rented in Ayrshire at a little fishing village called Dunure. He was there, of course, and both of his sisters, Jessie and Janet. I don't know why we considered ourselves immortal – the arrogance of youth, I suppose. But we worked hard and played hard, as it were. It was an extremely stimulating environment. We used to call it, of all things, the "Roaring Camp".'

'That's an odd name.'

'I think it was from a short story one of us had read about the gold rush in California called *The Luck of the Roaring Camp*. Dunure seemed a bit primitive to us – like a gold rush shanty town. But those weekends were truly beautiful. It was a lovely time for us all.'

'So, you were thrown together, you and Toshie?'

Margaret laughed again. 'Well, no. Not exactly. Toshie was engaged to John's sister Jessie. She had set her sights on him from the start, and I was the last person to think of coming between them.'

'And Toshie...? Did he return her affections?'

'Well, you know what he's like...'

Meg said nothing, waiting for Margaret to expand on her theme.

'He neither encouraged nor discouraged her. It was as if he accepted that they were somehow destined to be together and went along with it. I'm not sure he was ever in love with her, to be honest. He had asked John for permission to marry her, since their father was no longer alive, and John had told him they should wait until Toshie became better established.'

'And all this time you were waiting in the wings...'

'No, not really. It wasn't like that. We were like a family, like brothers and sisters, although there was never any doubt that Frances and Bertie would wind up together. Theirs was a match made in heaven.'

Meg wanted all the details, and decided to refill the teapot, excusing herself to the kitchen where she set the kettle back on the hob.

Left to herself, Margaret closed her eyes, allowing the memories of those summers to come flooding back. How they would take advantage of the long dry days to paint in the open air, and carry a picnic with them, so that work was always leavened with pleasure. She had often wondered if John's motives were slightly cynical because his employees would appreciate his generosity and pay it back with interest in terms of their loyalty. But even if that were the case, she realised how lucky they had been to be given the opportunity to draw and paint in that free and loving atmosphere.

They had been like young plants, nurtured and watered until they responded by issuing blooms infused with scent and colour.

* * *

'Don't you want to join the others?'

John had found Margaret in the bay window with an open book on her lap. He was wearing a floppy hat and carried a raincoat over his shoulder.

Margaret looked up and slipped a bus ticket onto the page. 'Yes, is everyone ready?'

'Ready and waiting. Frances has your paints. What's the book?'

'Ruskin. *The Seven Pillars*. You must have read it.'

'Of course. Essential stuff for architecture students. Is it Charles's?'

She offered him the copy, still open where she'd left it, and he noticed the little doodles down the right-hand margin in Mackintosh's unmistakable style.

'Ah. Are you reading it, or just looking at the pictures?'

Margaret shot him a dismissive look as she snapped the book shut. 'Come on, let's go.'

The rest of the self-titled 'Immortals' were waiting across the road, already laughing and joking in anticipation of a day's entertainment. Margaret's sister Frances had draped herself characteristically over Bertie McNair's shoulder, and Jessie and Jane Keppie were having a lively conversation with the three other girls. John was just about to lock the front door when he spotted the housekeeper coming up the garden path carrying an enormous basket of clean towels.

'Ah, Mrs Stewart. How are you today?'

'I'm right as rain, Sir. Thank you for asking. I'm sorry, I'm a bit late, on account of Mr Stewart was being a little cantankerous this morning.'

'That's perfectly all right. We're all out for the day now, so you can get on with your work undisturbed.' As he withdrew the key, he thought he'd better ask after her husband. 'How is Mr Stewart? Better, I hope.'

She made a face. 'He's just himself, Sir. A little prone to fanciful ideas. He thinks he saw the White Lady last night and now he can't stop talking about her. All in his imagination, of course.'

'Of course. Well, I'm sure you're a great comfort to him.'

As they took their leave, Margaret asked John what Mrs Stewart had been referring to.

'Oh, it's a local superstition. Kennedy Castle's supposed to be haunted and the White Lady is said to walk from the ruins at midnight across the park, and up across the raised beach. Actually, her route is supposed to go right through one of the rooms in the house.'

'That one at the back that you don't use?'

'Yes. Did you sense an atmosphere? Some people who've stayed here before refused to go in there, although they hadn't even heard the story.'

'No. I wasn't aware of anything,' said Margaret. 'I don't think I'm what they call... sensitive.'

'I'm sure you're a most sensitive girl in every way,' said John, holding the garden gate open for her.

'What do you have planned for us today?' she asked.

'Nothing too strenuous. Bertie wants to sketch some details of the mill at Dunure Mains – you know, stone skews and that kind of thing. My sister's armed with her camera, as usual.'

Margaret made a face. 'Oh dear. I hate having my picture taken.'

'Who said she was going to take your picture?'

'Jane always takes our pictures. The other day she said how boring it would be to have nothing but snaps of buildings.'

'Well, the camera's very useful in that respect. And I don't mind if she makes us all pose as well. It lightens the day.'

'The day,' said Margaret, 'is really light enough already.'

John never quite knew how to take her, but her remark wasn't intended as a rebuke – only to express how light-hearted she felt the moment she stepped outside and filled her lungs with the fresh country air.

John's other sister, Jessie, took Margaret's arm and walked with her at the rear of the little procession.

'I'm so glad you could join us,' she said. 'We're going to have such fun.'

Margaret said it was very kind of her brother to invite them all.

'Oh, you know John. Takes after our father in that respect. He loves giving other people opportunities.'

Her glance strayed to Margaret's sister ahead of them on the road, arm in arm with Bertie McNair. 'Look at Frances. I do believe she's in seventh heaven.'

'They're good together, aren't they?' said Margaret. 'Bertie's so full of life.'

'He's a devil,' said Jessie. 'She needs to watch that one!'

Kathy Cameron overheard them and turned round. 'Bertie's been teaching us the new dance.'

Margaret raised an eyebrow. 'Not the Kangaroo Hop? He made it up himself, you know. I don't think it's ever going to catch on.'

They all paused at the stile that led into the meadow. Charles said he was going to go to the mill with Bertie and John to sketch some details, and they would catch the others up around lunchtime. Frances asked Bertie if, by any chance, he had her smock.

'No, my dear. What would I be doing with your smock?'

'I don't know. I thought perhaps you'd brought it for me. I couldn't find it this morning.'

'Well, you must have mislaid it.' Giving a shrug, he caught hold of Charles's arm and they headed off with John towards the mill. The girls were left on their own.

'Did you hear about the White Lady?' said Frances. 'Apparently she "walked" last night.'

'Oh, that's just a lot of nonsense,' said Jessie.

'How did you hear about her?' asked Margaret.

'Bertie told me. He heard it from someone at the inn last night.'

'It's nothing but local gossip,' said Jessie. 'You shouldn't pay any attention.'

'Funnily enough,' said Margaret, 'that Mrs Stewart said her husband spotted the White Lady last night.'

'There you are!' cried Frances.

'What time did Toshie and Bertie get back from the inn last night?' Margaret asked, suspicious that they may have been up to some kind of mischief.

'Oh, I think it was well after midnight. Close to one o'clock, I should imagine.'

They turned their attention to Jane, who was trying to manoeuvre her camera and tripod over the stile into the meadow, and together they gave her a helping hand.

*　*　*

It was a warm, languorous morning. There were bees and dragonflies flitting across the hedgerows. The scent of ozone hung heavy in the air. Each of the artists found positions for themselves where they could be comfortable for the time it would take to produce a creditable sketch or painting. It was work, but it was relaxing work. As Margaret took inspiration from the looping tendrils of a white convolvulus, she remembered something Toshie had said about looking into the spaces between the foliage and making the shapes count.

She played with the idea of incorporating faces and was even tempted to introduce winged human figures. But suddenly the notion of it becoming like a childish puzzle – spot the fairy – didn't appeal to her. Instead, she started to draw human forms around the edge of her picture that were themselves elongated and sinuous, inspired by the forms of the plants.

Shortly after midday, they spotted the three men returning along the cliff top.

'Just in time for lunch,' cried Kathy, opening the hamper.

Agnes and Janet began to pass round the sandwiches they'd made earlier.

'So,' Jessie asked Charles, 'show me what you did.'

He had three pages of small thumbnail sketches. As Charles had said, they were details, noting how the building was put together.

'It's a fine building,' said Jessie. 'Why don't we paint the whole thing?'

'We shall,' Charles confirmed, biting into his sandwich. 'But we have to understand it first. It's like a language, you know? Almost a forgotten language. Incredible, isn't it? That the skill should get passed on from generation to generation, but it gets eroded on the way.'

'As does language,' said Jessie, appreciating his analogy.

'Yes, so we have to relearn it. Look at this.' He showed her how the gable stones rose beyond the ends of the gable, forming a series of steps – 'crow steps' – and the lead work that formed a little gutter – a 'secret gutter' – hidden behind those steps. 'They're decorative, of course, but primarily the steps make more sense than a slope. These days we agonise about how to stop the skew stones sliding down the slope, and here's the answer. No slope – steps. Simple, practical, beautiful.'

He smiled at Jessie, and she found herself thinking, 'Yes, like you. Simple, practical and beautiful.'

'We thought we'd go down to Maybole Castle next time, and Baltersan. There's much more of this kind of thing there.'

Jessie returned his smile, although she wished she had been invited. Then, seeing her brother making his way over to join them, she asked, 'How is the Art Club project going?'

'Well enough,' said Charles. 'Don't you think, John?'

John nodded. 'I've asked Charles to concentrate on the interiors. They're always a bit tricky. The committee wants panelling, but it's in danger of being too dark and you need to be able to set off each painting against its optimum background.'

'Have you seen the gesso work that Margaret's been playing with?' Charles asked. 'Perhaps we could commission her to work up something for the frieze.'

John wasn't so sure and glanced over towards Margaret, who was out of earshot. 'Let's see how it goes. I think we should keep it simple. I got the committee members to agree with me that plaster casts of the Elgin marbles wouldn't work, so I've already asked Bertie to have a look at a stencilled design instead. We need to have plain plaster between the dado and the frieze.' Spotting Margaret picking her way over across the heather to join them, he suddenly changed his tone, as if he wanted everyone to benefit from his wisdom. 'I reckon the Hornels will look best against plain white, don't you?'

Mention of the painter Edward Hornel, made Charles's face light up with enthusiasm. 'What that man's doing is incredible. Somehow, he makes the whole canvas a texture – I don't know, almost some kind of puzzle, with hidden shapes, interwoven with one another.'

'You like a bit of mystery in a painting, don't you?' Margaret teased him slightly.

'Well, I think he knows how to capture the popular imagination. Someday, Margaret, Hornel's pictures are going to be worth a lot of money.'

'Eddie's been to Japan,' said John. 'I think that's where a lot of his ideas have come from. He's invited me down to Kirkcudbright next weekend to see his studio.'

He managed to avoid eye contact with Charles who was looking at him hopefully, angling for an invitation to join them, but no such offer was forthcoming.

* * *

'Would everyone gather round?' Jane wanted to take pictures. 'Toshie. You in the middle. Janet and Kathy, make a frame around him. An archway... that's right. Frances and Agnes, you go behind Janet. Jessie and Margaret on the other side. There... nice and symmetrical.'

Margaret reluctantly did as she was bidden, but Jessie didn't want to turn her back on her. 'Come on,' she said. 'At least look as if you're enjoying yourself.'

'Oh, I am,' said Margaret, not wishing to appear ungrateful.

'Right,' said Jane. 'Bertie, where are you? You need to be in the front with Toshie. John, let's have you over here next to Jessie. Frances... what on earth are you doing?'

Frances had taken up a position around the back of everyone else and appeared to be trying to levitate.

'I am the White Lady!' said Frances.

And so they continued, recording the happiness of the day.

When the light was beginning to fade, they began to make their way back to the houses. Margaret caught up with Charles, and couldn't resist asking him, 'Do you know anything regarding the whereabouts of Frances's smock, Toshie?'

'Her infernal smock! What would I know about it?'

'I just thought you might know what Bertie did with it, after he'd finished with it.'

Charles stopped walking and gave Margaret a searching look. 'Did you ever think of becoming a detective?'

Margaret laughed. 'Why? Do you think I'm on to something?'

'What do you mean?'

'Well... what time did the two of you get back from the inn last night?'

'It was about midnight, I think.'

'And you must have had one or two drinks?'

'A wee hauf, or two.'

'And did Bertie get up to any high jinks?'

'Bertie was in his usual high spirits.'

'So, after you returned to the house, did he go back out?'

'He said he was too wound up to sleep. He needed to go for a walk.'

'In Frances's smock?'

'I'm sure I don't have the faintest idea what you're talking about.'

And that, as far as Margaret was concerned, was the nearest she was likely to get to a complete confession.

* * *

When Meg returned from the kitchen, she found Margaret asleep in her chair. Setting the teapot down on the side table, she gently touched Margaret's arm.

'Oh, I think I must have nodded off,' said Margaret. 'I hope I wasn't snoring.'

'No, you weren't. But what if you were? Who cares ...?'

'I care. I don't want to be sitting in your lovely drawing room grunting like a pig.'

Meg laughed. 'Come on, we're friends. We don't need to worry about being ourselves in each other's company.'

'You're very kind,' said Margaret.

'So... where were we? You were going to tell me about how you and Toshie finished up together. Of course, only if you want to....' She refilled both their cups from the teapot.

'It was Fra Newbery, really. You know, there are so many things we have to be grateful to him for.'

'He sounds like a remarkable man.'

Margaret nodded. 'Somehow, he realised straight away that if he put us together, something marvellous would happen. Frances and I were day students, and Toshie and Bertie attended evening classes; but that didn't stop him. He simply made the art school studios available to us in the evening, and the boys would come in and work with us after their class. And, well, as you know, we just clicked. We ended up spending a lot of time in each other's company.'

'He was a matchmaker!'

'Yes. Absolutely, as it turned out. But, of course, the match gave birth to so much more than our two marriages.' She reached over to the table and lifted her cup and saucer on to her lap. 'Father got a studio in Hope Street for Frances and me just before he died, and paid a year's rent up front. I remember Bertie calling in one day to see what Frances and I were working on. We were in the throes of designing posters for Joe Wright's umbrella company, and when Bertie arrived he started to poke fun at what we were doing. "How are the spooky sisters?" he asked us, the minute we opened the door.'

'Spooky? Why did he call you that?'

'It was the name we'd been given by people who didn't like our work. They couldn't understand the stylised way in which we had elongated the human form. So, they called us the Spook School.'

'I've had a bit of that kind of thing. From people who don't try to understand our art.'

'It's a shame, isn't it? They need to be taught to look – below the surface. To see past the obvious. Anyway, Bertie just had to seize the opportunity to tease us about it.'

'Didn't you mind?'

'No, not at all. You could forgive Bertie anything. You know, I think he actually gave us the idea for the name. He looked at the poster and said it needed a slogan. Then he said something like, "If they hadnae took it, they'd all be drookit!".'

Meg looked puzzled.

'"Drookit." It's Glaswegian. It means "soaked, drowned". I told Joe afterwards and he roared with laughter. Then he said "you know, that's not a bad idea. We could call it the Drooko." Afterwards he thought that didn't sound posh enough, so it became the Royal Drooko.' She smiled to herself at the recollection. 'Those were the days.'

'But Toshie wasn't there?'

'No, not at that point. He tended to spend a lot of time at his studio working on his own. But afterwards Bertie made us all go round to see what he was up to. We found him labouring over some furniture he was making for one of his fellow students – I think it was his first real attempt at doing so – and he was in the process of giving a chair its sixth coat of white paint. Bertie could never resist the temptation to poke fun at him. "Doesn't seem like a very comfortable chair to me," he said, and Toshie told him it wasn't meant for sitting on, which you can imagine just fuelled his derision. "Whatever happened to the idea that the form should be dictated by the function?" he wanted to know. "What use is a chair you can't sit on?"'

'And what did Toshie say to that?'

'Toshie told him rather sulkily that it was really a sculpture. A work of art in its own right. It was there to furnish the room, but there would be other chairs to sit on. And, of course, it was beautiful. I don't think I'd ever seen a crafted piece of furniture in which the form of the wood seemed so natural and harmonious. As if the chair had been grown rather than made, you know?'

Meg nodded. 'Yes, of course. I'm quite familiar with Toshie's furniture. I have an early memory of my mother taking me to the Willow Tea Rooms, and the place made such an impression on me. The magical white space was a haven from the drab greys and browns of Sauchiehall Street outside the window. I still insist on going there whenever we're in Glasgow.'

Finishing the rest of her scone, Meg brushed some crumbs off her lap. 'I take it Bertie's remarks didn't put Toshie's back up?'

'Toshie never took Bertie's jibes seriously. He knew it was just the way he was, and the reality was that Bertie admired his work. Which was why we all got on so well together.'

'But Toshie was also working as an architect at that time?'

'Oh yes, they both had permanent positions at Honeyman and Keppie. John had given Toshie the Glasgow Herald building to work on, and he threw himself into it body and soul. Sometimes I knew he wasn't really listening to what I was saying, because his mind was on something to do with the project. There was one time we'd taken a picnic into Kelvingrove Park, and we were all lying around on the grass. Jessie was there too, I remember. Bertie was expounding at length on the Hôtel Tassel that Horta had built in Brussels and how much he loved that organic decoration. But he wasn't getting any change out of Toshie. He kept saying things like, "Art Nouveau is clearly where we ought to be going, don't you think so, Toshie?", but Toshie was just doodling with a pencil on a corner of the tablecloth. He was drawing a thistle, beautifully, of course – you know how beautifully he can render botanical species. Eventually he just stood up and said, "No, I hate Art Nouveau," and then wandered off on his own.'

'But I thought...?'

'... that Toshie was an exponent of Art Nouveau? Not really, Meg. There are some things he has in common with that movement, but he sees it as too esoteric. Ornament for its own sake instead of an integral part of the form.'

She lifted her bag from the chair beside her, took out her handkerchief and dabbed delicately at the side of her mouth. 'Much later, when I saw the Herald building for the first time, I was looking at the water tower, and suddenly realised that the thistle that Toshie drew on the tablecloth that day was its inspiration. There was the thistle, built in stone.'

'It doesn't seem the most obvious connection.'

'No, but few people realise what a plastic material stone is, when it comes down to it. In the hands of a craftsman, the form isn't by any means limited to the rectangular shape of the blocks in which it comes from the quarry. Think of Michelangelo! Of course, Toshie was never a stone mason, but he could almost have been. He understands materials – stone, wood, steel or glass. It's one of his great strengths. He is a craftsman once removed.'

'The Glasgow Herald building must have kicked off his career, then.'

'Well, it should have done. You know our friend, Hermann Muthesius, in Germany? He greatly admired the building, and wanted to publish photographs of it in *Kunst und Dekoration*, but of course Toshie had to make a point of telling him that it could only be credited as the work of Honeyman and Keppie, and not as his personal work. It was just the way things were. But I'm sure Toshie always longed to be able to do work entirely for himself and claim it as his own.'

'So would you say he draws all his inspiration from nature?'

'He is shamelessly eclectic. Often, he draws on other historic buildings, with no scruples about incorporating a form that he admires. The best example was the church he designed at Garscube Road. St Matthews. He had made a drawing in his sketchbook of a church in Merriot when he was touring around Somerset – long before I met him. I wish

I could show you it. I think he still has that notebook. Perhaps next time you visit.'

'Yes, I'd like that,' said Meg.

'The church tower was tapered, resembling the pylon of an Egyptian temple and had a smaller six-sided tower hugging the corner, rising above the main tower like a chimney. Critics said he stole the idea, of course, but it was a master stroke, because the form of the 13th-century tower absolutely complemented the modern fluid lines of the main building next to it.'

'I'm sure Fergus showed it to me. Isn't it at that road junction? Queen's Cross?'

'Yes, that's it. I think it's a very fine building.'

'It's beautiful,' said Meg. 'We were lucky enough to be allowed to look inside.'

Meg got up and walked over to the window, where she stretched in a manner that demonstrated her background as a dancer. Looking out on the Chelsea landscape, she commented, 'Don't you miss Glasgow? London is so different, isn't it?'

'Very different,' Margaret agreed. 'Father was from Glasgow, but I grew up in Staffordshire. I think Toshie misses Glasgow more than I do. He feels most comfortable in the stone city of the Victorian era. You know, he was raised in Townhead in the north-east of the city, and it was one of those strange coincidences that the office was given the commission to build a school, right on the site where he was born. Of all the perspective drawings Toshie made of his buildings, those of the school are the only ones that show people – three little girls with skipping ropes by the school gates. I like to think that they were three of Toshie's sisters!'

'Goodness! How many sisters does he have?'

'Five. Two of them older, Bella and Martha, and three younger, Maggie, Ellen and Nancy.'

'You get on with them?'

'Not really. I think they consider me too posh and a bit "arty". There are no other artists in the family. Toshie had a brother, Billy, as well, but he ran off to sea when he was sixteen and was killed in South America.'

'Oh, that's sad.'

'Yes, but you see, having all those sisters explains a lot about Toshie. He was spoiled. They all ran around after him.'

'And does he expect you to do the same?'

Margaret laughed. 'He can expect all he likes.' Then she became serious. 'No, actually, he doesn't. If anything, he runs around after me.'

CHAPTER 3

THERE WAS THE sound of the front door being opened downstairs.

'Ah – they're back,' said Meg, getting up.

Seconds later, Charles and JD Fergusson swept into the room, their cheeks still aglow from the cold November air.

As Fergusson's wife lifted the tea things, Charles came up behind her and put his arms around her. 'How's my Meg?'

'Stop it, Toshie,' she squealed. 'You'll make me drop it!'

'Not at all. Your ballerina's sense of balance won't let you.'

'Well, the only *grand jeté* you're going to see is me throwing this tray at you!'

Fergus bent over Margaret and rubbed her shoulder. 'Nice to see you, Margaret.'

'So, what have you two been up to?' she asked.

'Wait till we tell you. Your husband's had the most marvellous idea.'

'Was it my idea?' said Charles. 'I thought you were the one who suggested it.'

'Well, whoever it was, I think it's something we need to pursue.'

'Sounds intriguing,' said Margaret. The boys exchanged conspiratorial glances, waiting until Meg reappeared from the kitchen, at which point Margaret told her, 'Fergus and Toshie have some plan they've been cooking up.'

Meg sat down next to her on the sofa.

'Go on...'

Margaret shrugged and made a gesture towards Meg's partner.

'You know those sheds the army has been trying to dispose of after the war?' asked Fergusson.

34

'The Armstrong huts?'

'The very ones,' he said. 'Some of them had been used as temporary barracks, but some are still as good as new.'

'Fergie's idea is to have them re-erected in Hyde Park and make them available to artists as exhibition space,' Charles explained.

'You know how Frank Rutter's been trying to set up somewhere that artists can exhibit in without having to jump through all the hoops that the Royal Academy insist on. And all the mainstream studios are too elitist and too expensive, so aspiring artists don't stand a chance.'

'Fergie found the caretaker at the barracks,' said Charles. 'He was a very helpful man and able to confirm that there are still no plans for them at the moment. It seems nobody else can think of a use for them.'

'So the next step is to go to the office of the Ministry of Works and see what they'll make of our idea.'

'What, now?' asked Meg. 'What about lunch?'

'No time like the present,' said Charles. 'Lunch will have to wait.'

'Well, we may not be here when you get back.'

'Do you hear that, Toshie?' said Fergusson. 'Our women have had enough of us. They're going to abandon us.'

'We'll be in the Blue Cockatoo,' said Margaret. 'Why don't you join us there afterwards?'

'Good idea. At least Hettie can be relied upon to look after the inner man.'

*　*　*

After an extended wait in the outer hall, Charles and Fergusson were escorted into the office of a Mr Underdone, who seemed to be in charge of the section dealing with requisitions by the War Office. Once seated in front of the official's huge mahogany desk, Fergusson outlined their plan for repurposing the huts in Hyde Park. Charles emphasised that the proposal was to locate the huts on the asphalt surface of the walkway, thus eliminating the need to replace any turf in the long term. He had hardly finished speaking when he was aware of an almost tangible air of scepticism.

'It's an excellent idea, gentlemen. I see one major stumbling block.' He paused for effect, offering them cigarettes – which both declined – then, lighting one himself, said, 'Money. There ain't none.'

'What we envisage should be able to be done on a shoestring,' said Charles. 'To all intents and purposes, everything is already in place. There's heating, lighting, conveniences. Very little would need to be spent.'

'Paintings and sculptures need light. Have you thought about that?'

'We would use daylight to reduce the running costs,' said Charles. 'We propose to take off the asbestos on the north-facing side of the roofs and replace it with glass.'

'You would have to engage an architect,' said Mr Underdone.

Fergusson sighed. Evidently, he hadn't been listening. 'Mr Mackintosh not only *is* an architect, he is a very distinguished architect. He is a fellow of the Royal Institute and very well-respected north of the border.'

Mr Underdone was unimpressed.

'No doubt you know of the Glasgow School of Art,' said Fergusson.

'Unfortunately, our interests do not extend as far as Scotland.'

'Then, Liverpool Cathedral.'

Charles shot Fergusson a look and coughed. Even if the official was aware of the building, it seemed doubtful that he would have known who its architect was, or that its design had been the subject of a national competition, or that Mackintosh's entry to the competition had been declined.

'Well, at the end of the day, it's not up to me,' continued Underdone, clearly losing interest in the project. 'The War Office would have to be consulted, since they would have the final say. If you wished to approach them directly, I, for one, would not stand in your way.'

Of course, Mr Underdone knew as well as his guests that, for the general public, there were no routes into the War Office aside from himself.

* * *

The two men were not yet ready to impart their lack of success to their wives. Spotting a bar as they walked along Knightsbridge Road, Charles made a suggestion with no more than a twitch of his shoulder. They ordered pints of bitter before installing themselves in a booth where they could lick their wounds.

'There are two kinds of people,' declared Fergusson.

Supping the foam off his pint, Charles agreed. 'Those who think there are two kinds of people, and all the rest.'

Fergusson laughed. 'Those who see the world in all its many layers, all its complexities and possibilities, and...'

'And all the rest,' said Charles. 'Like our esteemed Mr Underdone.'

'Who see nothing but the immediate problems and their most obvious solutions.' Following Charles's lead, Fergusson took the head off his drink. 'But you must have encountered more than your fair share of those types in your time.'

'Huh! Present company excepted, I could count the others on the fingers of one hand.' And he proceeded to do so. 'Fra Newbery, now there's a man of vision.'

'Erstwhile Director of the Glasgow School of Art.'

Charles nodded. 'My mentor. My lifelong friend.' Another swig of his drink, and another finger. 'Kate Cranston.'

'A woman of substance.'

'A woman of refined taste and perspicacity. She *knew*, Fergie. She was investing in more than herself. She contributed to Glasgow's culture. They were more than just tea rooms. She gave Glasgow the very thing it was waiting for to make its society tick, and she knew exactly how to make them into places that made people comfortable and captured their imaginations.'

'Was she a supporter of the temperance movement?'

Charles laughed. 'No, she wasn't trying to get the working man out of the pub. She was providing a pub for the working ladies – and the non-working ladies. Somewhere to meet other than in each other's front parlours.'

'And it worked. So, who's next?'

'William Davidson.'

'The man for whom you built the house at Kilmacolm?'

'The same. You see, he understood what we were about. His neighbours told him his house looked austere – like a prison – but he ignored them all. He was actually prepared to suppress his own ideas and tastes in the pursuit of something bigger than himself.'

'His house was bigger than he was? It must have been enormous!'

'Windyhill had to be big enough for his family.' Still smiling from his friend's little joke, Charles became slightly dewy-eyed. 'He has a lovely family. His three children used to call me "Uncle Tosh". You know, when the first turf was cut in Kilmacolm, William insisted on having a ceremony and laid on a bottle of the best bubbly. He even got me to design a special goblet for the occasion and we had it made by the local silversmith. I'm afraid we all got a bit merry. You know what a building site's like, and with this damned foot of mine...'

'You fell over?'

'Flat on my face. The kids thought it was a huge joke. And, as if that weren't bad enough, when Christmas came round, William had me play Santa Claus at their house party and the cotton wool on my costume caught fire from the candles on the Christmas tree.'

'My goodness, were you all right?'

'William dragged me outside and pushed me into the lily pond by the front door to put out the flames. I always seemed to end up on my back in front of those children.' He knocked back the rest of his drink. 'I must get in touch with Hamish,' he said, 'and ask after his father.'

'That's three.'

'Walter Blackie, of course. Built the Hill House at Helensburgh. Some of my critics said I'd designed a monument to myself – but it's a monument to art. To the ability of one man to see beyond the fashions of the day. Like one of your paintings, Fergie, the house speaks for itself by virtue of its visible qualities – but it also has one great invisible quality.'

'Its soul.'

'Precisely.'

'Number five?'

'There aren't more.' Charles gave his friend a look of resignation. 'That's about it.'

Lighting a cigarette, Fergusson decided to play devil's advocate. 'Damn it all, Toshie. What you say is all very well, but you're seeking special privileges. If some man of dubious taste commissions a painting from me, and doesn't like what I give him, he can give it away to his daughter, or hang it in his toilet. He doesn't have to live in it. You want a client that will give you free rein, but he has to live with the consequences.'

'Yes, I know. That's why architecture's such a bloody awful profession. We are supposed to be whores, Fergie. We have to flatter them and give them what they want. My old partner John Keppie can do it, which is why he's a successful architect. But I'm not able. Never have been.' He produced his pipe from his pocket. 'I had a commission in Killearn, to the north of Glasgow. Auchenibert House, for a family by the name of Shand. It was a lovely site – had a lot going for it.' He lowered his voice again and glanced quickly over his shoulder in case the Shands were in the bar. 'They wanted mock Tudor.'

'They had the wrong architect.'

'Oh, we got so far down the line and some of it was fine, but as the build proceeded I couldn't stomach what they wanted to do. So, in the end, I suggested they get somebody else to finish it for them. And that's precisely what they did!'

'Well, you have to be true to your art.'

Charles gave an ironic snort. 'Oh, that's so high-flown. It's really just a disability, like this damned foot. That's why I really want to walk away from it all – or limp away, if I have to. I'd rather just paint you a picture that you could hang up in your toilet.'

'Well, you're a damn fine painter, Toshie. You could do worse.'

'The thought scares me a little. You can't practise architecture without clients, but it's possible to paint for nobody but yourself, if you have a mind to.'

'I frequently do.'

'And you sell...'

'As would you. You've already sold some of your work.'

'That was Margaret. She made me plead with Davidson to buy some of my flower paintings from Walberswick. We needed the cash to pay the rent. It was practically charity.'

'Nonsense. The man has taste, you said so yourself. He'll value those paintings.'

Charles sat back in the booth. 'You know, I think he will. But listen, Fergie, compared with Margaret I'm a rank amateur. I acknowledge I have a talent of sorts, but Margaret has genius.'

'I believe you're right. Margaret's gesso work is inspired. And the graphic style that she and her sister have developed is quite exquisite.' He offered Charles a cigarette.

Shaking his head, Charles knocked his pipe out in the ashtray and refilled it from his pouch. 'So what can I do? I suppose I could always try my hand at sculpture.'

Fergusson smiled. 'I've been having a go, but it's not easy. There's a bigger investment both in time and money. Sometimes it just doesn't work. You know how it can be with painting – how sometimes your *idée fixe* just refuses to appear on the canvas, no matter how hard you try.'

Charles nodded.

'So you can abandon it, paint over it, whatever. When a sculpture doesn't work, you're left with the raw materials.'

'Not as bad as when a whole building goes off the rails.'

'Come now, that's never happened to you, surely.'

'Well, no, not the whole. But large elements can be frustratingly disappointing, no matter how fine your intentions were at the outset.'

'But we all make mistakes. Wasn't it you who said, "There is hope in honest error..."?'

'"... None in the icy perfections of the mere stylist." Well remembered, Fergie. Only I didn't say it. It's a quotation from JD Sedding. I just embroidered it – not literally, of course.'

'I've seen it – what would you call it? – your icon. It's very fine. I admired the way you had taken the words and made a picture out of them with that uneven organic style of lettering of yours, and formed them in a square.'

Charles gave a modest shrug. 'It seemed a good maxim to adopt.'

'So, my "honest error",' said Fergusson, 'is an unfinished work of art, like Schubert's symphony.'

'Which is why you've got that massive lump of Carrara marble sitting in your parlour?'

'Huh! If only...! Doesn't it just make you take your hat off to the likes of Michelangelo?'

He paused, a million miles away in his thoughts. Then he decided to share a particular case in point.

'One time when Meg and I were in Antibes, she'd gone off shopping and I was waiting for her in this little bar where someone had told me it was worth trying the local absinthe. The house across the road had a grey gable with green shutters and there was a very tall plantain growing alongside. You know what these trees are like? They're very interesting. Where the bark peels off the branches, they're almost flesh coloured, and it's amazing the way the branches compose themselves. They're so old... so full of time. I was fascinated by it. But it's just a tree, and it just takes its time to do what it does. It doesn't flash or scintillate, this old plantain. It accepts its friend, the sun, and absorbs it, making beautiful patterns on the ground – truly wonderful. There is form, colour, depth, shade, dignity, friendliness, protection and comfort, of course. But on top of that, there's something else – a tremendous lot more, in fact. I just sat still and looked, and it appeared that nothing was happening. But something was happening – just very slowly.

'So, it gave me this idea, and when we got back to London, I went to the wood yard and bought a four by four batten, seven feet long. With the idea of the plantain still in my mind, I took my pencil and drew two intertwined lines on one side, like the movement of the branches. Then I put it in that corner of the room, by the dresser, where I could see it nearly all the time. It's been there for about two years now and I've never been able to get a start on it. But it's only a lump of four by four. Not quite Carrara marble!'

*   *   *

They found Meg and Margaret at their usual table in the Blue Cockatoo.

'How did you get on?' asked Meg, as the two men settled into comfortable armchairs.

'Not well,' said Fergusson. 'We're in the hands of fools and philistines. Basically, they don't want to know.'

'Are they aware who they were dealing with?' asked Margaret.

'Fergie said I was the architect of Liverpool Cathedral,' said Charles. 'Not that it made any impression on the man. I don't think it would have made any difference at all if I'd been Giles Gilbert Scott himself.'

'He said we need to consult the War Office,' said Fergusson. 'I'm not very optimistic. We'll go and see them, of course, but it was strongly suggested that the park belongs to the King, and that would be the end of it.'

Hettie came over to ask if they wished to order something to eat.

'I could eat a horse,' said Charles.

'Sorry,' said Hettie, with a smile. 'I'm afraid we don't have any at the moment. There's still rationing, you know.'

They settled for some sandwiches and a pot of tea for four.

* * *

'So, what took you to Walberswick?' Meg wanted to know, after they had cleared the decks.

'We'd been there a lot,' said Margaret. 'The Newberys often rented a cottage there, and they asked us to join them on a number of occasions. After all that unpleasantness with John Keppie, when Toshie withdrew from the partnership, we felt we needed to get away from Glasgow for a while, and Walberswick was the obvious place. If there hadn't been all that bother with the military, we'd probably still be there. Technically, we're barred, both of us, from ever setting foot in East Anglia, although Toshie's been back a couple of times.

'But the Newberys weren't there at that time?'

'No, they were in France. Otherwise we would probably have shared a cottage.'

'They sound like nice people,' said Meg.

'They are,' said Margaret. 'I told you we had Fra to thank for setting us off on the right road at the Art School along with Frances and Bertie. He and his wife have remained our friends. We have so much to be grateful to him for, not least for putting us in touch with the leading figures in the Secession Movement in Vienna; Hoffman, Klimt, and the others. He knew how much we would have in common with them – a shared dislike of the art establishment with their academic snobbery.'

'But your name was never associated with the new building of the Glasgow School of Art, am I right?' asked Fergusson.

'My name was kept out of it,' said Charles, 'but that was all right. It's only as it should be. The commission was with Honeyman and Keppie, and at the time I was a mere employee. Individuals never get credited for their contribution.'

'But it was all his work,' said Margaret. 'The project was carried out in two phases, and when the first of those was completed, Toshie wasn't even given his place in the opening ceremony – or any place at all, come to that.'

'To be honest, I preferred it that way. I couldn't be doing with all the hoo-hah. All these worthies, spouting forth on a subject about which they knew very little.'

Margaret knew that this was Charles's modesty speaking – that he had felt his exclusion from the credits very deeply, and still resented it even now.

'Toshie got the last laugh, though,' she said.

'How so?'

'Francis Newbery had done a painting – a portrait group of the School's building committee – and he requested permission to present it as a gift to the board. They were Toshie's "worthies", all seated round the table, looking very learned and serious.'

'Fra called them "The Moles",' said Charles.

'I've seen that painting,' said Fergusson.

'Then you'll know what he did. After the committee had approved the painting, but before the official unveiling, he added another figure to the composition.'

'You mean, he put you in the frame, Toshie? You weren't in it originally?'

'Well, of course not. I was only the architect.'

'Fra actually had to add an extra strip of material to the side of the canvas,' Margaret continued. 'Consequently, when they unveiled the picture at the ceremony, it wasn't quite what they expected to see. There was a bit of nervous coughing and one or two red faces, but, of course, nobody could say anything, and it was too late to do anything about it. The portrait hangs in the boardroom to this day, and there's Toshie in his rightful place!'

Meg clapped her hands. 'How wonderful! What a delightful man that Fra Newbery is!'

* * *

The following weekend, JD Fergusson was sitting in his parlour smoking and trying to work up sufficient enthusiasm to take himself up to his studio and continue with the canvas on his easel, when there was a knock at the door.

'What ho, Fergie, old man!' Charles was standing on the doorstep holding a flowerpot from which grew two intertwined twigs with two leaves at the top, and two more near the bottom. 'I saw this on a barrow in the market, and something about it made me think of you!'

Fergusson was bemused and stared at the plant for a moment wondering what had possessed his friend. Suddenly, he burst out laughing. 'My plantain!' he exclaimed.

'Well, a pathetic excuse for one. I think it may have found its way into a shipment of bananas.'

'Come in, come in. Meg!' he shouted, 'Toshie's here!'

They shared a pot of tea, and after Charles had gone, Fergusson started to draw Charles's plant, noting how the stems intertwined, and began to get the feeling that he'd done this before. Then, retrieving his piece of four-by-four, he discovered that the pencil lines he'd drawn on the batten exactly mirrored the line of the plant.

He'd needed fresh motivation, and Charles's plant had provided it. Fergusson picked up his pencil and marked out a more developed line, shading in the areas that needed to be removed. Then, he took it out to his workshop and made a start with the chisel. And like a phoenix, *The Dryad* slowly rose from the almost abandoned batten.

CHAPTER 4

'IT'S GLORIOUS HERE, isn't it?'

Meg breathed deeply, filling her lungs with the fresh morning air. Since their men had gone off to meet an official from the Ministry of Works, the two women had taken the opportunity to go for a walk in Hyde Park.

'We don't get out often enough,' said Margaret. 'I think we have a tendency to imagine that time's too precious to waste doing nothing.'

'We're not doing nothing,' said Meg, stretching and embracing her personal space in the arc of her arms. 'We're seeking inspiration from nature.'

Margaret also took a deep breath. 'You're right. We need to take something in before we can give something out – be creative, I mean.'

Meg looked at her and shook her head. 'We shouldn't even need to justify ourselves. This should be part of our weekly routine.'

'But then it might not hold the same allure for us, strange creatures that we are. We need novelty.'

'Where else would you go, if there were no barriers?'

'Oh, I don't know,' said Margaret. 'Somewhere warm, I think. The South of France, or Spain, maybe.'

'Italy?'

'Toshie has mixed feelings about Italy – he seems to think there is something very artificial about Florence. But I haven't completely given up hope of persuading him to take me to some of the places he did like.'

'Fergus and I had such wonderful times in Antibes. Wouldn't it be jolly if we could all go there together?'

'I told you about our weekends in Ayrshire, didn't I?' said Margaret. 'It could be like "The Roaring Camp" all over again.' In her mind's eye, she pictured herself with Toshie on some bluff above the sea, sitting with their easels, while Meg danced around them abandoning herself to the natural environment.

They had come to the bridge over the Serpentine and paused to watch a courting couple pass below in a boat, the young man in his shirtsleeves pulling hard on the oars. Meg was reminded that, at the time Margaret was referring to, Charles was still engaged to Jessie Keppie. Glancing at her friend and seeing a flicker of emotion that might indicate she was having the same thought, she took the opportunity to ask how it came about that the couple decided to break off their engagement.

'Well, the thing was, I wasn't there when it happened. I only heard about it afterwards from Bertie, and he got it from someone else. You know how it is with gossip, so I didn't know the full truth of it, and I never asked Toshie because it was really none of my business. But poor Jessie – I think she'd begun to feel as if she was flogging a dead horse, if that's not too cruel a metaphor.'

They walked on in silence for a bit, before Margaret felt able to expand on the story.

'Jessie must have been getting quite desperate, because at one point she actually wrote a wee fairy story and got it published in the student paper. It was all about a princess who was waiting for the king's consent to marry her prince – the king would have been John Keppie, of course. But the prince had been placed under a spell by a pair of witches, and she was imprisoned in a circle of fire, or something like that. It seemed obvious to everybody at the time that she was just airing how she felt about Toshie, and I guess I was supposed to be one of the evil witches.'

'Didn't you mind?'

'No, not at all. I just felt sorry for her.'

'So she must have done something to bring the situation to a head?'

'No, I think it was Toshie's fault, really. They'd gone off to some "do" at the tennis club where Jessie was a member. Toshie hates those kinds of events. He never dances, of course, because of his foot, and in those days it made him feel awkward and self-conscious. From all accounts, he might have been overdoing the liquor. Bertie reckoned that, as well as the wine they were offering, he probably had a hipflask in his pocket and was helping himself to nips of whisky on the sly. Maybe even in the gents' toilet.'

Meg laughed. 'What are they like, these men?'

'Then, apparently, the band called for couples to come on to the floor for 'Strip the Willow'.'

"Strip the Willow'...?'

'It's a very energetic traditional dance where the men and women form two lines, and each couple dances from the top of the column to the bottom, birling around with each of the men or women in turn. It's very good fun and usually quite exhausting.'

'Like 'The Grand Old Duke of York'?'

'Yes, very similar – maybe a little more boisterous. Anyway, Toshie surprised everybody by dragging poor Jessie onto the floor, and got really into the spirit of the thing, birling her around in quite the style. As I understand it, when the first set ended everyone else left the floor, exhausted; but the band kept playing and Toshie and Jessie continued to revolve in time to the music – which just shows how much he must have had to drink. According to Bertie, they got faster and faster until Toshie just let Jessie go. Of course, she shot off across the room and collided with a table, knocking over the chairs, and no doubt spilling some of the drinks. It must have been a terrible blow to that poor girl's dignity!'

Meg nodded, imagining only too well the scene that Margaret had described.

'People were screaming and the band stopped playing. Toshie just remained standing on his own in the middle of the floor. Then some man got up and told him in no uncertain terms that he was "nothing but a cad". But Toshie had nothing to say in his own defence – seemingly he just uttered something like, "Sir, you're right. I'll drink to that!" and flung his empty hipflask on the floor. So, I think that must have been the last straw for Jessie, because it wasn't long after that event that they broke off their engagement.'

'That can't have gone down very well with Toshie's boss.'

'No, and it didn't exactly help their relationship at work. Actually, John Keppie encouraged Jessie to sue for breach of promise, but she didn't want to do that. It wasn't in her nature. I think she was quite resigned and just suffered in silence.'

'And then you and he…?'

'Well, no, it was some years after that. We just got gradually closer over that period. I mean, we worked together a lot. Frances and Bertie were already very much an item of course, so we always made up a foursome with them. I suppose it was what they call a "slow-burner".'

'But, in the end, it became very powerful.'

'And, obviously, still is!'

* * *

When they reached Marble Arch, Margaret suggested they go somewhere for a refreshment.

'What about Alan's Tea Rooms?' said Meg. 'It's not far from here.'

The two women proceeded along Oxford Street until they arrived at the place where, before the law was changed to allow women the vote, the suffragettes used to hold their meetings.

'Will this do?' asked Meg, holding the door open. 'I don't suppose it comes up to Miss Cranston's standards.'

'It's fine,' said Margaret. 'We probably don't come up to Miss Cranston's standards either.'

Meg thought that was doubtful, at least in Margaret's case, for she seemed to her to be exactly the kind of society lady who would be very much at home in Glasgow's exclusive tea rooms.

They paused at the hat stand while Meg slipped out of her long coat, before shaking her body like a cat coming in from the cold. Margaret decided to leave hers on, but reached up to extract the long silver pin that secured her wide-brimmed hat to her luxuriant red hair. Choosing a table near the window, the white tablecloth adorned with a little china vase of freesias, they ordered a pot of tea and some scones and then sat back to enjoy the experience of being waited upon.

Margaret found her friend's company very relaxing. It was amazing how Meg managed to draw her out to talk about things that she normally kept to herself, or between her and Toshie.

'Tell me,' Meg asked her, leaning forward slightly as if she didn't want their conversation to be overheard, 'how was it that the four of you became so well known on the continent? Was it really all down to Fra Newbery's introducing you to the Secession Movement?'

Margaret could detect her friend's ambition. Britain was already too small a place for her to express her talent. She wanted to know how to spread her wings, and there was a world out there, waiting for her. Margaret was quite sure that Meg could blossom in the European atmosphere that she and Charles had come to love, and didn't mind at all that she was blatantly putting out feelers.

'I can't remember if I told you about Gleeson White. The editor of *The Studio*? You must have seen it.'

'Yes, of course.'

'Fra put us in touch with him and he published an article about us in the magazine. Among other things, he said that the work Frances and I were engaged in was ahead of its time, blurring the distinction between art and architecture, and perfectly complemented Toshie's projects. He expressed the view that those who were laughing at us today would be eulogising us a few more years down the line, although I couldn't imagine what made him think so. He seemed to have the gift of being able to predict future trends.'

'The power of the press...' said Meg.

'Yes, exactly. Fortunately for us, the magazine was distributed in France, Germany and Austria, so it meant that it would be read by both artists and architects – they don't make the distinction there that we do here. Anyway, there must have been something in our work that struck a chord among students and lecturers in Germany. The next thing we knew, Hermann Muthesius and his friends were coming over to see us, and that was the start of a very close friendship with Hermann.'

Something that she recalled made her laugh as in retrospect it seemed a little absurd. 'You know, Meg, he even asked Toshie to be a godfather to his son Eckart, along with Fra Newbery. I'm not sure that either ever fulfilled their roles in that respect!'

Meg's own journey in the world of the arts had given her a degree of insight into how things worked. 'It must have been very frustrating for Toshie not to have the same degree of recognition here.'

'I don't think it bothered him initially. He just thought that, in time, as he worked his way up the ladder and established his own practice, he would have greater influence. He supposed that the rest of the establishment would come around to his way of thinking.'

Their waitress returned pushing a trolley from which she unloaded a silver teapot and matching pot of hot water, a milk jug, a sugar bowl and a three-tiered plate of scones and cakes. Finally, she placed a little saucer on the table containing fluted curls of butter and a single ice cube.

'Ah, the loneliness of the artist,' said Meg. 'It's never that easy.' She took one of the scones from the cake stand, sliced it in half and buttered both sides. 'But his partnership with Keppie? Surely he must have received some encouragement there?'

'He should have, shouldn't he?' Margaret hesitated a little before helping herself to a cream slice. 'But they were pulling in separate directions. John Keppie was following the safe and respectable path of giving his clients what they knew and liked. Toshie, as always, wanted to push the boundaries – and inevitably he wasn't commanding the same level of fees.'

'But the School of Art? It must have been a tremendous boost for the practice?'

'For the practice, yes. But it was as if everyone conspired to play down Toshie's contribution. Remember I told you he was hardly acknowledged at the grand opening of the first phase.'

'Oh, yes of course. Didn't Fra Newbery literally put him back in the frame?'

'Yes, but even during the second phase of construction things weren't much better. He was continually criticised for overspending and for taking decisions without his client's consent – which was probably true, but then they simply didn't, or couldn't, respect his genius. So gradually he lost heart. The spark went out. I felt so helpless. There was nothing I could do or suggest that would make any difference, and Toshie started avoiding me, staying in the office all night. He relied on a bottle of scotch for company.'

'Poor Toshie,' said Meg. 'And poor you.'

'It was at times like that I really missed having Frances around.' Margaret poured some milk into her cup before topping it up with tea. 'There are still times I wish... but never mind, we can't change things, can we? She loves Bertie, and Bertie loves her, so in the end that's all that matters, isn't it?'

'Didn't they go to Liverpool?'

'Yes, Bertie was offered a job there before they got married, in the University College. He'd had a successful show at the Gutekünst Gallery in London just before that, and one thing led to another. He wanted Frances to move down there with him then, but the family talked her out of it. You know, the usual thing: wait till Herbert gets established, a little money under his belt. All that sort of nonsense. To be honest, I think Mother hoped the whole thing would fizzle out once they were apart, but I knew that was never going to happen.'

'So how did Bertie get on in Liverpool? Did he do all right?'

'At first, yes. He was teaching design and stained glass in a jumble of old buildings by the railway cuttings. They called them the Art Sheds. He was very popular with his students – he has such a winning personality, of course.'

'And then they got married.'

'My brother Charles arranged the whole thing for them in Dumbarton. By that time, the family was reconciled to the fact that they were made for each other and had realised there was no point in kicking against it. So, of course, Frances went to live with him in Liverpool.'

'But you still saw a bit of them?'

'Oh, yes. We had some wonderful holidays with them in Scotland. They would bring their bikes up on the train, and we used to cycle around Loch Lomond with them.' Margaret smiled at the recollection. 'We found the most delightful little cottage one time in the wee village of Luss. Absolute perfection.'

'And they had a son?'

'Mmm, Sylvan. They brought him up to Scotland as well, to show him off.' She smiled at the memory of that holiday, and the tiny boy clinging to Frances's waist on the back of her bicycle.

Meanwhile, Meg seemed to be struggling to remember something.

'You know Augustus John, the artist?' she asked. 'He's quite friendly with Fergus. I've a feeling he told me that he knew them.'

'That's right, he did. He was one of the tutors at the School of Architecture and Design where Bertie was working. Of course, the two of them disagreed fundamentally on matters of art, but, despite that, they got on all right with each other. Frances and Bertie entertained him and his wife – I think she's called Ida, isn't she? – to dinner at their home and they had a lovely time together, although I don't think Augustus John was terribly impressed with their house.'

Margaret topped up the teapot and refilled Meg's cup to the brim. Mention of Augustus John had triggered an association that made her breezy manner cloud over for a moment. 'You know, something happened around that time that changed Bertie's attitude to life. Toshie stayed with them when he was working on his submission for the competition to design Liverpool Cathedral, and Bertie told him he was furious that his class had been moved out of the Art Sheds to some other location in Liverpool that didn't suit him so well. That must have been just before Charles Reilly, who was head of the department, terminated Bertie's employment. Did you know he was Toshie's *bête noire?*'

'Oh? What did Toshie have against Professor Reilly?'

'It's not really like him to fall out with anyone, but Toshie blamed Reilly for not placing him in that competition. He wanted the commission so badly, and still considers he was unfairly treated. Just think what that would have meant.'

'Yes, of course.'

'Reilly also changed the focus of the Liverpool school to a more traditional approach, and that resulted in some of the students forming a breakaway.'

'The art establishment strikes again!'

'Exactly. The students set up the Sandon Studios in competition with the University, and Bertie joined them, but it didn't work out for him. So, a couple of years later he and Frances moved back to Scotland with Sylvan, who was seven years old by that time.'

'You must have welcomed that, having your sister back?'

'Of course, but the problem was, Bertie couldn't get any work. He applied for a post at the School of Art – and they turned him down. Can you imagine? When we were there, he was one of the leading lights. Frances got herself a job as an assistant in the embroidery class, but they were being encouraged to design for the sewing machine, and that didn't suit Frances at all, so she resigned. And, as they had no money between them, they ended up living with Bertie's family in Ayrshire. So, you see, they weren't really back in Glasgow.'

'Couldn't your brother have taken them in? Wasn't he living in a castle?'

Margaret laughed. 'Well, although it was called a castle, it was really just a big house. But space wasn't the problem; it was Bertie's drinking. He was never one to moderate his habit, but, of course, because his self-esteem had taken such a blow, it only got worse. And his own father wasn't any more tolerant. He eventually sent Bertie off to some place on the Isle of Man to dry out! When he came back, he discovered he'd been disinherited, and my brother finally took pity on him and Frances while they looked for somewhere to live. So, for a while, the four of us were back together, but it wasn't anything like the old days. They were both shadows of their former selves.

'But at least Bertie had given up the drink?'

Margaret made a snort of exasperation. 'No, not really. The Isle of Man venture seemed to have been a failure. The next suggestion was that he go off to Canada to find work, but I'm sure the real motive was to get him out of my family's hair.'

'Did he go?'

'He didn't have much choice. My brother was prepared to make sure Frances and Sylvan had a roof over their heads, but not if Bertie wasn't making any sort of effort. My uncle David had a flat in Gibson Street in Glasgow, and when my aunt died it made sense for Frances to move in with him. Then, out of the blue, Bertie re-appeared from Canada, having failed to find work, and then, as they say, the fat was well and truly in the fire!'

'Who on earth says that? I would have said, "all hell was let loose!"'

Margaret gave her friend an old-fashioned look. 'Well, however you say it, that's what happened. That was when I made the trip up from Walberswick to try and sort things out, although goodness knows what I thought was going to happen, or what I could do about it.'

'We can never sort out our family's problems. We can only support them.'

Margaret sat back in her chair and placed her hands in her lap.

'I'm afraid that's true,' she said.

CHAPTER 5

TO BE HONEST, Meg, my first inkling that I meant any more to Toshie than a companion and fellow artist came when he took me to see the flat he was thinking of renting in the city centre. Up until that time, he'd been living in the east end of Glasgow in a semi-basement room in Firpark Terrace that belonged to his father. It wasn't that he was looking for my opinion as to whether or not he should take the flat, because it was obvious from his eagerness that he had already made up his mind. After all, the location was perfect, only minutes from the offices of Honeyman and Keppie, and the price was well within his means. But he was so energised, I could tell there was something special about it that appealed to him and he wanted to share whatever it was with me.

It was on the corner of Bath Street and Main Street, accessed from the latter via a common stairway. There were three rooms: a living room, a bedroom and a kitchen big enough to dine in. But, of course, it was the living room that had caught Toshie's imagination. It had two very large windows, facing north – perfect light for an artist – and a third in the corner facing west. I can still picture him clearly, standing in the middle of that room telling me how he envisioned altering its proportions.

'What do you think, Margaret?' he asked me, his eyes burning with enthusiasm. 'Do you think it will work?'

I was never in any doubt that it would. But he kept saying, 'We could do this, we could change that,' until eventually I asked, 'Who is this "we"?'

Whereupon he took my hand and said, 'Margaret, you don't think I can do it all on my own, do you?'

My heart leapt. It was the first time he had ever acknowledged my contribution to his work in so many words. But I made no reply; I didn't want to say anything that would sound presumptuous.

'Look,' he said. 'We could take away the picture rail and make another one, lower down, but continue it right across the windows. It would render the scale more human, more intimate. What do you think?'

I teased him that he could always resurrect the frieze of cats that he'd put around the walls of his basement room. He laughed at that. The idea had really come from Bertie, who had created a similar effect in his own room with stencils of mermaids all round the top of the walls. I recalled him saying that he'd spent even more on drawing pins than he had on watercolours!

'Cats?' said Toshie. 'I was thinking sirens; beautiful, slender, red-haired women.' And, placing his hand on the back of my neck, he gently lifted my hair before teasing it out of the ribbon with which I had tied it up that morning. I remember scolding him for undoing my efforts and tried my best to restore order to my coiffure.

But I knew exactly what he was talking about, because we had already done some work of a similar nature on my family's house in Bowling, just outside Dumbarton, and I suppose that was what laid the foundations. It was so exciting: the thought of doing it for himself this time, to be his own client, as it were. So it became a joint project, and he couldn't have made it clearer that I was to be an equal partner in any decisions. We transformed that living room beyond recognition, making it double as a working studio and incorporating a long, low, white fireplace similar to the one at Dunglass, but this time we placed a cushioned shelf on either side – one for each of my cats. We painted the walls white, gave it a pale grey carpet and brought in the best pieces of Toshie's white furniture.

Of course, work on the flat had to be paid for, and although Toshie had devoted most of his spare time to it, there were occasions when he was obliged to stay late in the office. All his efforts to date had been in the design of the new building for the Glasgow Art School, but now that the first phase of the development had been formally opened, he was able to concentrate his efforts on getting consent from the Dean of Guild Court for the Daily Record building off Renfield Street. Oh, and then there was Kate Cranston, who had asked him to design a luncheon room for her tearoom in Ingram Street. But the thing that really fired his imagination was Windyhill – the design for the Davidsons' house at Kilmacolm.

Sometimes, as we were working together on the flat – applying yet another coat of white paint to the walls or the ceiling – he would say to me, 'It's very difficult, you know, Margaret, the relationship between the lounge and the dining room. Really when you're trying to design someone else's living space, you can never be really sure whether they think the same way as you do, although William and Jean come quite close.'

I think he had slightly fallen in love with that family, and they with him. There were some evenings when I was working alone in the flat, painting in the little lilac details with my small brush, and he would turn up at eight or nine o'clock, tired but excited. 'I think I've got it now,' he would say. 'William's going to be so impressed tomorrow. You know, Margaret, that man is such a pleasure to work for.'

*   *   *

After we'd had some of our work published in Europe, Kalas the art critic came across from France to pay us a visit. He was most impressed with what we had done to the flat. He described it as 'an amazing house of white and violet', the work of 'two visionary souls in ecstatic communion.' He also said some very nice things about Toshie. I still have the article here:

> ... A gentleman thirty-five years old, dressed all in black, with long dark hair parted in the middle; the eyes slumber in their setting below bushy eyebrows, flaming up from their gloom in occasional flashes of varicoloured sparks; the mouth betrays caution, perhaps timidity – probably mockery. He dresses in black, and so the general appearance is of a clean-shaven American clergyman who is still pulsing with the emotion and travail of his last metaphysical discourse, but has succeeded, by powers of restraint, in preserving an impassivity and unnatural silence.

Later on that year, Hermann Muthesius also paid us a visit and said that he liked the flat very much.

'But Margaret,' he said, 'you can't really be going to live here?'

I didn't know what he meant. 'Hermann,' I said, 'are you concerned that Toshie and I are not husband and wife?'

He gave me that lovely apologetic smile of his, and said, 'No, of course I don't mean that. Who cares about some piece of paper that you and Herr Mackintosh may or may not have!'

'So...?'

'I mean it's too perfect. Everything is too ordered, too much in its place. What would happen if I were to lay a book down on this table? You would have to tell me to pick it up immediately.'

'Yes, I probably would, Hermann. Books should go on bookshelves, clothes go in wardrobes and food goes in the larder.'

'Yes, yes, yes. But where do you... live?'

'Why, here!'

'It's too perfect, Margaret. The world is not ready to live like this.'

There seemed to be a gulf between us, at least as far as what a house should comprise. I couldn't quite believe that Hermann existed in the squalor that he claimed, nor could he reconcile himself to the idea that Toshie and I could relax in our environment. He even seemed to think that Toshie dressed the way he did so as not to clash with what he called our 'minimalist interiors'.

* * *

When the flat at Main Street was finally finished, Toshie removed the last vestige of whitewash from the windowpanes and joined me where I was standing on the newly laid carpet.

'Well, it's ready to move in,' he said. 'I suppose we'd better get married.'

I don't think he meant to be so casual. It was typical of him to expect me to read between the lines. Part of me wanted to chide him for being so damnably unromantic, although, in a way, it was very romantic, because it was so in keeping with the way he was. So, I just put my arm around his waist and took his hand in my other hand, and then we danced a waltz on that pale grey carpet, both of us hearing the same invisible music and neither of us caring about his poor lame foot.

When we stopped, we sank down on the floor and lay there for a while, side-by-side. Then I said, 'I will be happy to be your wife. We have so many interests in common.'

I shall never forget his reply.

'Margaret, I have only two interest. You first, and then my work next.'

We were married in St Dunstan's Episcopal Church in Dumbarton on the 22nd of August 1900. The day was wet and windy, but it felt as if the sun was shining. All my family were there, and Toshie's father and all his sisters and their children. Then everybody came back to the flat. Toshie's nephews and nieces were very sweet, but I don't think I'm very good with children. He and I were so worried about our precious carpet, we both spent half the time stooping down surreptitiously to pick up crumbs from the floor. We'd given them meringues, which possibly wasn't the best idea.

For our honeymoon, we went to Holy Island – what an enchanting place! Of course, Toshie took his sketchpad and rendered the scenes around him with a magical touch that gave them the esoteric quality of a fairy tale illustration. It was never anything more than a pencil line on paper – no shading or hatching or colour washes – but his pencil always seems to have a will of its own and his sketches came to life because of it.

We enjoyed Holy Island so much that we returned the following year, and the year after that with Frances, Bertie and my brother Charles. I suppose that was the nearest we ever got to resurrecting the spirit of the 'Roaring Camp'.

*　　*　　*

We were beginning to feel like the 'Famous Four', because by this time Charles, Bertie, Frances and I were becoming known in Europe. It was the beginning of the new century and we were all infected by the excitement that stemmed from so many new possibilities. Fritz Wärndorfer, one of Hermann's friends, came over to pay us a visit and was so impressed with the flat that he asked us to design a music salon for his house in Vienna. That was our first project in Europe. It was pretty much on the same lines as our living room, but considerably larger – big enough to accommodate his grand piano – and I produced a number of gesso panels for it on themes inspired by the playwright and poet, Maurice Maeterlinck. Fritz was extremely kind to me, but something of a flatterer.

He called me a 'most distinguished lady' and claimed that he was acquainted with no other ladies of my ilk. Anyway, he was very pleased with how the room turned out and published an article about it in *Kunst und Dekoration*.

Hermann Muthesius also wrote a very positive article about us in the same magazine and then invited us to come over to Austria to meet members of the Vienna Secession, which he could arrange through the university. So Frances and Bertie decided to accompany us, along with George Walton and our friend Talwin Morris. George is an architect, and has his own interior design company that specialises in stained glass. He had done some art nouveau panels for one of Kate Cranston's tearooms.

We were met at the railway station by a bunch of students who told us they had a carriage waiting for us on the street to take us to the campus. We couldn't believe it! But when we walked out of the station and saw the carriage parked at the side of the road, there was no sign of any horses.

Toshie put his hand on the shoulder of one of the students. 'So... you have some horses somewhere...?'

The student laughed and said, 'No, we are the horses!' And they threw garlands of flowers over us before picking up the shafts of the carriage and propelling us through the streets of Vienna as if we were royalty.

Of course, they knew that Toshie had been the designer of the Glasgow Art School, even though officially it was accredited to Honeyman and Keppie, and that helped quite a bit to make up for the lack of recognition he received for his work in Scotland, though he was always typically modest about his contribution.

* * *

One year after our marriage, John Keppie made Toshie a junior partner in the office, so it became the firm of *Honeyman,*

Keppie and Mackintosh, and his new status increased his confidence. The practice moved to an office in Blythswood Square, still very close to the flat – in some ways perhaps a little too close, because it was easy for Toshie to return there in the evening if there was some design detail on his mind that he wanted to explore on the drawing board.

It was around about that time that the practice was approached by Walter Blackie, the publisher, who expressed an interest in building a house for himself near the Firth of Clyde, based on what he'd seen of William Davidson's house at Kilmacolm. It was no coincidence that our friend, Talwin Morris, was artistic director in Blackie's at the time. Walter said he liked Windyhill so much that he was sure Toshie could do something along similar lines for him, though possibly a bit larger in scale.

It was to become one of Toshie's favourite projects and he grasped the opportunity with eager hands. The site was high on a hillside in Helensburgh, surrounded by other salubrious mansions overlooking the River Clyde. It was another one of those collaborations that he completely enjoyed – Blackie's a man who knows his own mind, but doesn't close it to advice when it comes from a professional that he trusts. The result was a Scots baronial mansion, but on a more intimate scale and with magical touches reminiscent of the castles in Arthur Rackham's beautiful illustrations.

Those were the best times. Toshie was on the crest of a wave. His long-term client, Kate Cranston had acquired more premises and had us both remodelling the interiors for her Willow Tea Room in Sauchiehall Street. And because the school at Townhead had been such a success, the Glasgow School Board invited the practice to design another school, this time south of the river in Scotland Street, to which Toshie responded with another unique *tour de force*. It had some of the magic of the Hillhouse with its glassy stair towers and must have been a delightful environment for both the pupils and the teaching staff. At the same time, Toshie was continuing to receive recognition in Germany. A long, illustrated article about the Hill House appeared in *Kunst und Dekoration*, in which the writer was particularly enthusiastic about the bedroom. He said that:

> ... in the middle of this great white symphony we find ourselves surprised by the melodious rhythm of the stencil painting, regardless of whether we look at this wonderful bedroom from its alcove, or turn towards the fireplace or the mirror. The ideal relationship of the floor to the ceiling is achieved not only by the ornamental motifs of the stencils, but also the ascending shapes of the furniture, the descending shapes of the light fittings, and the mirror in its perfect harmony with its white surroundings.

That room would capture the imagination of any woman. Naturally, Mrs Blackie loved it, and so did I. In my opinion, it was a bedroom fit for a fairy princess, and I suppose I must have said as much to Toshie. Although I wasn't especially given to envying his clients for the spaces he designed for them, perhaps something in the way I admired the Hill House continued to play on his mind, for two years after that article was published he took me to see a house in Florentine Terrace, just up the hill from Glasgow University. He showed me round without saying very much, until finally I remarked that it clearly held a lot of potential. Who was it for?

'Why,' he said, 'for us, of course.'

I should have known. He had barely managed to suppress that twinkle in his eye that I had come to love, and I don't know how I missed it on this occasion.

'Can we afford it?' I asked.

Grinning now, he said that he thought that we could.

Well, naturally, that changed my whole perspective, and I had to go around the place again looking at everything in much more detail, only this time with the Hill House bed-room at the back of my mind. We were both thinking in terms of what we had done with our existing flat, but whereas at the Main Street flat we had struggled to alter the perceived proportions of the room, here we already had dimensions of a less lofty, more intimate scale. With a little work and a lot of imagination, we could easily transform this terraced house into a home fit for an architect and his artist wife. And so we created another white living room for ourselves that beau-tifully complemented the other apartments in the house – a splendid dining room, and a bedroom almost as magical as the one at the Hill House. The years we spent in Florentine Terrace were the happiest of our married life.

* * *

That was in 1906. By that time, the practice was occupied with the second phase of the Art School. Fra Newbery, of course, always knew that the project was in the capable hands of his star pupil and continued to be Toshie's cham-pion whenever there was a clash between his aspirations and the narrow-minded restrictions of the building com-mittee. Nevertheless, the strain on Toshie was beginning to show from his sustained effort of battling with those petty members. They argued about details of the library on which he absolutely refused to back down. One such dispute was whether the gallery should continue around all four sides, which Toshie absolutely insisted that it did. He won that particular argument, thank goodness. But there were many other such disagreements, and the committee rubbed him up the wrong way by complaining to John Keppie that a lot of the work was unauthorised and extravagant. A year or so later, Fra and his wife called round to the flat one evening.

'What about taking a break?' Jessie suggested. 'You know we have a cottage in Walberswick. We're going down there again for a few days next week. Why don't the two of you join us?'

Toshie was reluctant at first, but finally gave in to our joint persuasive powers. We spent a marvellous long weekend there – it was the first time that either of us had been to Suffolk. The atmosphere on the coast reminded us of those wonderful summer days we spent in Dunure, and Toshie found it greatly relaxing to paint the wild flowers that he came across in the dunes and the hedgerows.

Finally, things at the Art School calmed down and the second phase opened on schedule. The governors declared that they were completely satisfied with the result. As, by all reports, did the students, who found it a delightful place in which to work. That should have been no surprise, since it was designed by one of their own number.

*   *   *

Toshie had been a partner in the firm for thirteen years by the time John Honeyman retired, and things began to go downhill. The work that John Keppie was bringing in was lucrative, but none of it appealed to Toshie. The kind of clients with whom he was prepared to collaborate tended not to pay as well, and even they were becoming thin on the ground. The wonderful Kate Cranston gave us a bit more work at her tea room in Ingram Street, but it wasn't enough to keep him on a par with John's side of the operation, which inevitably led to both parties harbouring resentment: for John, that Toshie wasn't pulling his weight, and for Toshie that John was selling out to an inferior quality of architecture.

Matters came to a head when the practice undertook to submit a competition entry for a teacher training college at Jordanhill on the western outskirts of the city. Toshie agreed to undertake the design, but he could hardly motivate himself to engage with the project. He had started going out of the office at lunchtime and not returning until the middle of the afternoon, and there was always a bottle of whisky within easy reach of his desk. Although he would make up his time by staying on late, I began to think it was more from a desire to avoid confronting me than to do any actual work. Then, only a week before the entry was due to be submitted, there was a general panic when they realised that Toshie had produced virtually nothing of any use. John had to engage Graham Henderson to salvage the situation, otherwise Honeyman, Keppie and Mackintosh would have had no entry to submit. As it turned out, Graham won the competition for them. It became inescapably clear that Toshie was suffering from depression and his position in the office was unsustainable. So, by mutual consent, he and John dissolved their partnership in 1913. Toshie initially practised from home, although he toyed with the idea of setting up an office for himself in the Bath Street premises that Honeyman and Keppie had occupied previously. But his depression, together with his drinking, began to tell on his physical condition, and his health deteriorated alarmingly. It wasn't long before we had to summon the doctor who, on sounding Toshie's chest, shook his head and diagnosed pneumonia. This required complete bed rest. Toshie would have to stop working altogether and we had to rely on what little I made from my fabric designs and embroidery. Eventually, when he was well enough to travel, Fra Newbery came to our rescue once again by suggesting that we should both head back to Walberswick.

'With all this talk of war at the moment, there's no point in sitting around waiting for something to happen. It doesn't sound to me as if Asquith has any hope of brokering peace. There's no work around at the moment, anyway,' he told Toshie. 'The cottage is lying empty. It's the perfect place to recuperate. You can take it for as long as you need.'

So we closed up the shutters at Florentine Terrace, and headed south again. And that was really how we found ourselves embarking on the journey that brought us here to London with the prospect of a whole new life outside of Glasgow.

I'm not sure we've found it yet, but just maybe, Meg, there's a possibility that Toshie and I can move on from here. Who knows where we're going to end up?

CHAPTER 6

MARGARET HAD SET the table for breakfast and was sitting reading the paper, waiting for Charles to join her. Now that the war was over, there was a daily diet of better news to be absorbed, which was proving an enjoyable way to start the day. Sunlight streamed in from the little courtyard, filtering through the leaves of a plane tree that stood outside the window. She looked up as her husband shuffled into the room, still yawning, and running a hand through his unkempt hair.

'Good morning,' he said, sleepily.

Margaret asked him what his plans were.

'Miss Elder's coming round. I'm going to see if she can come up with some ways to save money on Harold's studio.'

Harold Squire was an artist that they had come to know through their group of friends in Chelsea. He had bought a plot of land within a stone's throw of the studio that the Mackintoshes were renting.

Charles took a seat at the table. 'Have you finished with the paper?'

Folding it neatly, Margaret placed it beside his plate. 'How's Hero shaping up?'

'I don't know if she's going to be much use. Ana Berry said she trained at the Slade. Well, she can certainly wield a pencil, but she doesn't seem to have much idea about building.'

Ana was one of the leading lights in the Arts League of Service who had expressed an interest in Fergusson's now abandoned Hyde Park project. The league was still looking for studio space for their members, however, and Ana had approached Charles along with her colleague Eleanor Elder with a view to his designing rentable studio spaces in Chelsea. Hero was Eleanor's sister.

'You can only become experienced by getting experience,' observed Margaret.

'I was going to put her to work on the artist studios, but I'm not sure she's up to it.'

'Why not? If she's an artist herself, she'll have insight into how they should work.'

'As a client, yes. But can she make the leap into bricks and mortar?'

Margaret asked what the brief was.

'It's rather different from Harold Squire's. His studio will be just for himself, but the Arts League want to build studio spaces that can be rented out at reasonable rates to young artists or the men who've come back from the war. Although most of them try to work in their own homes, nine times out of ten the light's all wrong, and, as you know, you can't always leave your work lying around until you finish it.'

'No, and they couldn't have their wives making gesso panels on the white carpet.'

Charles ignored her teasing remark, which was untrue anyway, as, when they were in Glasgow, Margaret had always retreated to the attic of their house in Florentine Terrace when she was about to do something messy.

'Ana Berry has asked Meg if she can hold a public meeting at her club to see if she can drum up some financial support.'

When Miss Elder arrived an hour later, Charles took her round to his office at Glebe Place. He showed her the drawing of Harold Squire's project, which was taped to one of the drawing boards, and could tell she was impressed by the sheer ambition of it. Although the site was narrow and restricted, the proposal was for a deep plan on three floors, with the studio occupying a double-height space on the first floor. There was living accommodation on the ground and first floors, and a sunroom and garden on the roof.

'He wants to get the price down to six thousand pounds,' said Charles.

'Oh. That might be a tall order.'

'Quite. I thought you might have a look at the floor areas and work out how much we can afford on a pro rata basis.'

'I'll have a go.'

Charles was not hopeful. He had given her the exercise to do, because it would tax her brain rather than her eye. He wanted to see if she could distil the essence of Harold's two-gallon brief into a pint pot, but he was afraid that it was asking the impossible. He went over to his own drawing board and perched on the stool. There, he turned his attention to the adjoining site, where the Arts League hoped to erect their studios for rent. Along with Harold Squire's proposal, the combined project would occupy the whole corner of Glebe Place and Upper Cheyne Row – quite an imposing addition to the Chelsea streetscape.

* * *

Two days later, Hero Elder knocked on the door of Charles's office and opened it a fraction. 'Mr Squire is here,' she whispered through the gap, 'and Mrs Claude.'

Mrs Claude was Harold Squire's sister, who, it had now become clear, was funding the project.

'Come in, come in,' called Charles, drawing two chairs up to his layout table. 'We have a revised proposal for you to look at.'

The proposal wasn't so much revised as truncated. Gone was the cluster of interlocking spaces that so characterised the first scheme. Now it was a house with a studio attached at the rear, although many of the features had been retained that were typical of a Mackintosh design. Nevertheless, Harold was delighted.

'It has something,' he said. 'A magnificence, that no other studio in London can lay claim to.' He took some time to peruse the drawings. 'And how much do you reckon this can be built for?'

'I think around six thousand,' Charles confirmed.

Mrs Claude looked aghast. 'Six!' she cried. 'But we only have four!'

Charles said nothing. He simply took up his 2B pencil and drew a heavy diagonal line across the first floor.

* * *

Winter had set in. With the darker mornings there was less incentive to get out of bed, and, with few clients, Charles was in no hurry to get to his studio. When the doorbell tinkled, Margaret sat up in bed.

'It's the postman, Toshie. Maybe he has a parcel for us.'

Charles took this as an instruction to go and open the door. He put on his bathrobe and shuffled downstairs, returning with a sheaf of letters and a telegram addressed to Margaret, for which he had had been obliged to sign.

'It's from Bertie,' she said, wondering what on earth would occasion a communication from him rather than from her sister. Tearing open the seal, it took her seconds to grasp its significance.

'Oh, Toshie. It's Frances. She's died.' She let the telegram drop to the floor and began frantically pacing around the bedroom. 'What on earth can have happened? She wasn't even unwell...'

Charles picked up the telegram and read the words, 'cerebral haemorrhage'.

His wife looked at him with her mouth open and then, as if the truth of the words had suddenly hit home, her legs collapsed from under her, and he scarcely managed to catch her before she fell. With the weight of her now in his arms, he felt her whole body shake and tremble while he did his best to soothe her, gently stroking her long tresses.

When the initial shock subsided, she went through to the bathroom and bathed her face. 'I shall have to go to Glasgow. Today, I think. I'm sure there's a train.'

'Shouldn't we speak to Bertie first? We could make a telephone call from the Cockatoo.'

'No, I have to go.' She had found a suitcase and was stuffing clothes into it, aimlessly, without thinking. Suddenly she froze. 'Oh, Toshie. I can't believe it.'

He held her again as another wave of anguish overtook her.

'Would you like me to go with you?'

'No... there's no sense in shelling out for two train fares.' Then she had a thought. 'You can come in the taxi with me to the station. I might need your shoulder again.'

*　*　*

When Charles arrived back at his office there was a deputation of five men in dark suits waiting for him.

'Mr Mackintosh?'

Charles confirmed that it was he they were looking for and hoped they hadn't been waiting long.

The leader of the party introduced himself as the Chief Planning Officer for the Burgh of Chelsea, and explained that his companions comprised the committee of the Ecclesiastical Commissioners and their surveyor, one Mr Clifton.

'Mr Clifton has been engaged to report on the Arts League project to the ground landlords. Naturally, he wished to visit the site and would appreciate if you would explain the salient aspects of the proposal to him.'

Charles nodded his acknowledgement of Mr Clifton. 'You are welcome to visit the site,' he said, 'but you must allow me a little time to put a presentation together. Now is not a good time. We have just been informed of a family bereavement.'

Sympathies were expressed and, having fixed a time for Charles to come to Cheyne House the following week, the little group shuffled off to inspect the adjoining site, for which, as representatives of the ground landlords, they hardly needed Charles's permission. Charles entered the office, picked up his pencil and waited for inspiration, but the morning's news, together with the thought of his looming confrontation with the Ecclesiastical Committee, filled him with gloom.

As it turned out, no amount of groundwork could prepare him for the onslaught. At the appointed hour, he arrived with a number of drawings mounted on board, and took a few minutes to lay them out on the board room table before presenting the proposal to the sceptical-looking committee members before him.

'The Arts League of Service,' he explained, 'is a non-profit-making public organisation, whose aim is to assist artists to find spaces in which to work. As you know, the requirements for painters, sculptors and the like can be quite onerous, not least in quantity and quality of daylight. I believe my involvement in the Glasgow School of Art uniquely qualifies me to design a building of this nature.'

There was a general murmur of approval, after which Mr Clifton asked, 'And what exactly was your involvement with the Glasgow School of Art, Mr Mackintosh?'

Charles gave him a weary look. 'I was the architect. The Glasgow School of Art has established an international reputation and is exceedingly popular with its students in regard to the spaces provided for their work.'

'I see,' said Mr Clifton. He whispered something to a colleague, and Charles was sure that he overheard the words 'Honeyman and Keppie', which resulted in the colleague eyeing Charles with a sceptical look. Then Clifton sat back with his arms folded, while Charles led the committee through the various features of his scheme.

Finally, when Charles resumed his seat, it was the surveyor's turn to stand.

'What you say is most interesting, Mr Mackintosh, but my superiors are expecting that the building about to occupy this site be graced with certain architectural features, which are notably absent from the proposal before us.'

'What sort of architectural features do you have in mind?' asked Charles, struggling to disguise the disdain in his voice.

'I mean, for one thing, ornamentation. Without it, I'm sure you'll agree, the whole thing is too flat, too dull. You would need to provide it with a few swags here and some swirls there, to lift the thing above the pedestrian. This is Chelsea, Mr Mackintosh. We expect certain standards. This...' he indicated the drawings with a sweeping gesture, 'is not architecture.'

Ignoring the final remark, and wondering if Clifton would spot the implicit irony, Charles asked if the addition of a few frills might render the proposal acceptable to the committee.

'There are other problems with this,' said the surveyor, 'not least of which is that it is too modern to fit well into this mature and historic environment.'

'Then, may I speak directly to the Board,' suggested Charles, 'to try and convince them of the merits of this scheme?'

Mr Clifton sighed. 'No, you may not. They have engaged me for this purpose, and they will accept my word on the matter. As it stands, I cannot see my way to recommending this proposal to the Board for acceptance. And without their acceptance, there will be no planning consent.'

'Then, good day, gentlemen.'

Charles left Cheyne House, feeling numb. The events of the last week seemed to have drawn a cloud over his and Margaret's lives, and he took himself off to the Blue Cockatoo in the hope that he could cheer himself up in the company of like-minded friends. JD Fergusson and Meg were already there, and Meg came rushing over to the door the minute she spotted him.

'Charles, come and join us. Where's Margaret?'

Charles explained that his wife had gone to Glasgow for Frances's funeral.

'Oh, Charles, we can't tell you how sorry we are. We were devastated to hear her news, weren't we Fergus? Please pass on our sympathies to Margaret when you're speaking to her.'

Fergusson shook Charles's hand and helped him into the seat beside him, patting his upper arm.

'How are you bearing up, old chap?'

'Oh, you know,' said Charles. 'I always miss Margaret terribly when she's away.'

'If you feel up to it,' said Meg, 'you must come to the theatre tomorrow. We're having a dress rehearsal for the Christmas Show, and I've asked a number of the club committee members to come along. I need you to have a look at the backdrop. I'm not sure if it's quite right.'

'I've already told her what I think,' said Fergusson. 'But what I think isn't that important, apparently.'

'Fergus, you know how much I value your opinion. But wouldn't it be foolish to have the world's greatest architect as a friend and not to take advantage of his infinite wisdom?'

Fergusson mimicked Meg's tendency to sycophancy. 'Perhaps the world's greatest architect has something better to do tomorrow.'

'I'd be delighted to go,' said Charles. 'I've been meaning to drop in for ages.'

'Good,' said Meg. 'We're kicking off at midday.'

'Anyway, I've got some news for you,' said Fergusson. 'You just missed the illustrious writer. He was asking after you.'

'Shaw?' George Bernard Shaw had frequently been at the Blue Cockatoo during their gatherings and Charles was sorry that he hadn't been there to talk with him. 'What was he saying for himself this time?'

'He's been up to Northampton. Just back, as a matter of fact. You'll never guess where he was staying?'

Bemused, Charles shook his head.

'At Derngate, with your client, Wynne Bassett-Lowke! He put Shaw up in the bedroom you designed.'

Refilling his pipe, Charles sat back in his seat. 'What was the illustrious writer doing in the house of a man who makes toy trains?'

'Oh, he and Wynne go back a long way, apparently. Shaw is something of a hero of his. You know Wynne is a man of breeding when it comes to the arts.'

'Well, he has good taste in architects.'

'Quite. But GBS was there for a specific reason. You're not going to believe this. Bassett-Lowke was having him sculpted.'

'A sculpture of Shaw? What? For his garden?'

'No, for his model railway.'

'Isn't it just too delicious, Charles?' said Meg, thrilled at being able to share this titbit with her friend. 'You know how these people who have model trains make the most exquisite miniature villages, with everything to scale? I think they call it "O-gauge". Now, of course, you have to put people on the platform, don't you, waiting for the train? So, he's going to market a range of little painted lead figures. You can already buy those things, only his are all going to be models of real famous people. It's going to be his "personality range". He should do you as well, Toshie.'

'To be honest, that wasn't the only reason Shaw was there,' explained Fergusson. 'His latest play is on at the Northampton Royal Theatre, *Arms and the Man*.'

Meg ignored the interruption. 'You're going to have to buy yourself a set of people, Charles, and the next time you make a model of one of your buildings, you could have George Bernard Shaw standing outside. Wouldn't that lend it something of an air of gravitas?'

'Perhaps that's what I need for the Cheyne Walk Studios. The figure of GBS standing there might just convince my man Clifton that this is a work of architecture.'

Fergusson and Meg detected that this was something of a sore point.

'Who's Clifton?' asked Fergusson.

Charles told them about his brush with the landlords' surveyor.

'Fools and philistines,' said Fergusson. 'Isn't it always thus?'

'I tell you, Fergie,' said Charles, 'if I can't get this one past the powers that be, I've had it with architecture.'

'Then what would you do, Charles?' asked Meg.

'I'd take up painting. I wouldn't be anywhere near as good as Fergie, but I'd have a damn good try.'

'I keep telling you, Toshie, you could do worse.' He pulled out a cigarette and lit it. 'But listen, man, I never told you what Shaw had to say about your house at Derngate.'

'Go on...'

'Well, apparently Bassett-Lowke apologised for the décor, and said that he hoped that the illustrious writer would not be kept awake by the rather striking striped wallpaper.'

'And what did the illustrious writer say?'

Fergusson affected a Dublin accent. 'Sure, that'll be no problem at all. I always sleep with me eyes shut.'

For a moment Charles stared at him in disbelief, and then began with his infectious laugh that soon had his friends laughing along with him. Their hysteria was something of an antidote to the dismal events of the week.

*　*　*

At twelve o'clock the next day, Charles pushed open the door of the former billiards hall that Meg Morris rented for use as a dance studio and theatre. The makeshift stage was already set for the performance and the backdrop lit with some of the new electric lights. The backcloth seemed to have drawn inspiration from some of Margaret's designs and Charles thought that the interpretation was a reasonable effort, although it had been executed in quite bright, vibrant colours.

Meg was on the stage having a conversation with Loïs Hutton, one of the dancers. Charles took a seat five rows back from the front and intended to watch unobserved, but when she'd finished her conversation with Loïs, Meg glanced over and spotted him.

'There you are, Toshie. What do you think of the backcloth?'

'I think it's excellent,' he said. 'But I do have a little worry. It's so colourful and eye-catching that you might risk your audience focusing on the backdrop instead of the dancers.'

'Ah, good!'

'Good? You mean you don't mind if the dancers disappear into the background?'

'They won't disappear, Toshie. But the whole idea is that the dancers' costumes and the backcloth work together. They become one: an integral work of art. Do you see?'

Charles could see what she meant, but reserved judgement.

'Can you stay and watch the rehearsal?' Meg asked him.

'Absolutely. I mean to.'

As the preparations began to coalesce towards a beginning, another figure slid into the row of seats beside Charles, and he recognised his fellow committee-member Eugene Goossens.

'Hello, Mackintosh,' said Eugene. 'Meg's cornered you for a free consultation, then?'

'Just my opinion of the backcloth,' whispered Charles. 'Actually, Margaret's verdict would have been more valuable, but she's in Glasgow.'

Eugene gave Charles a meaningful stare with one raised eyebrow. 'I believe she also wants to discuss your design for the new theatre. The committee is assembling after the show.'

'I'll be happy to help in whatever way I can,' said Charles.

The programme comprised a number of short pieces in the barefoot rhythmic style that Meg had developed along with Loïs Hutton. The two men were especially impressed by an item entitled 'Ancestral Fear', a *mimodrame* by Loïs's partner Hélène Vanel, in which the emotion of fear was expressed through a combination of music, costumes and mime. And Toshie could see now exactly what Meg had meant. It was as if the backcloth came alive as the dancers emerged from it.

Afterwards, Charles and Eugene joined Meg in her small office.

'Well, Toshie? Did you like our show?'

'Superb, Meg, as always. Of course, I know nothing about dancing... but as a piece of art, it seemed flawless to me.'

'You know very well, because you're always telling me, that painting, architecture, music and dancing can all be judged by the same standard.'

'Well, then, you have my judgement. Just don't take any notice of anything Fergie says.'

Meg laughed. 'Now, your plan for my theatre. Could you spare a minute or two?'

Eugene gave Charles a look that said, 'I told you so.'

Charles said, 'For you, Meg, I could spare three. Just so long as you don't want to change anything.'

She reached for the rolled-up plan that was sitting on a shelf behind her and spread it out on the desk. 'I thought we could possibly use that store at the back of the auditorium as a projection room. Do you think that's practical? Cinema has a great future and it could bring in some money for us. But as well as that, we could incorporate moving images in our presentations, couldn't we? Wouldn't that be an amazing effect?'

Charles had to agree that it not only sounded feasible, but was an exciting idea.

'Plus, we need a revolving stage. That's not too much to ask, is it?'

'You can have anything you want, Meg. All you need is the wherewithal to pay for it!' He reached into his pocket, pulled out a tiny model figure, and placed it on the plan, facing the stage. 'Perhaps you can persuade Mr Shaw to put on one of his plays!'

'Oh, Toshie. You got one! How absolutely delightful. Thank you so much!'

She picked up the model and placed it on the shelf, before rolling up the plan.

'There we are. The Margaret Morris Club. Patron: Mr George Bernard Shaw.'

'You will have to ask him.'

'I'll ask him. Do you think he'll agree?'

Charles smiled. No man ever turned down any request from Meg.

CHAPTER 7

AS SOON AS Margaret stepped off the train from Glasgow at Euston Station, she spotted her devoted husband waiting for her at the barrier. After handing the inspector her ticket, she put down her case and, without saying a word, allowed him to cradle her in his arms, oblivious of the other travellers pushing past them.

'How I've missed you, Toshie,' she said.

'Margaret, I've missed you every minute of every day.' He kissed her again. 'Welcome back. How was it?'

'It was awful. I still can't get over it. Bertie was devastated, of course, and my brother – I've never seen him looking so distraught.' She wiped her eyes. 'There's a possibility Frances might have taken her own life.'

'Oh, no! Is that what they think?'

'It's what my Charles thinks, and of course he blames Bertie, privately, at least. But nobody else has said anything. They've closed ranks, I think.' She took out her handkerchief again. 'She was so young. Only forty-eight. Oh, Toshie, if only I had been there!'

'But you couldn't. You could never have watched over your sister's every move.'

'I know. It's just, if that was her state of mind, I might have been able to help.'

'Dear Margaret. If she had asked for your help, of course you would have done whatever you could. But she never did.'

Margaret suddenly drew herself upright, wiped her eyes again and put her handkerchief away. 'You're right, of course. We shall have to get on with our lives, so we don't have a chance to brood.'

'That's what we'll do,' said Charles. But at the back of his mind was the disaster of the Cheyne Walk Studios, suggesting that there wasn't so very much in his life to get on with.

When they got back home, after they had eaten, Charles filled Margaret in on what had taken place with Clifton the surveyor.

'If it's any consolation,' said Margaret, 'I've a feeling that the Arts League and Service are never going to be able to raise the funds anyway. I shouldn't spend too long on a revised proposal – they might not be able to pay your fee.'

'Meg's still talking about building her theatre, but I fear she might not be able to raise enough either. The cost of building anything is becoming extortionate. What you could build for four thousand pounds before the war would now set you back almost three times that amount.'

Margaret appeared distracted and, getting up, walked slowly over to the window.

'I think I'd better let Miss Elder go,' said Charles. 'We're not going to be able to pay her. In any case, she doesn't really do anything.'

'I think...' said Margaret, staring out at the garden. 'I think we'll throw a party.'

Charles cast an admiring glance at his wife. There she was, still reeling from Frances's death, and already talking in terms of entertaining. Margaret was an aficionado of the house party and Charles knew from experience that she would relish every opportunity to design the event as a piece of theatre, paying careful attention to the arrangement of the tableware and napkins, the positions of the chairs, the flowers and even, if necessary, re-arranging the pictures on the walls. The overall effect was similar to the one that she and Toshie had achieved for Miss Kate Cranston, and on more than one occasion she had already recreated in the tiny Glebe Place Studios something of the atmosphere of those luxurious Glasgow tea rooms. Consequently, Margaret's parties were among the most popular intimate social functions in the Chelsea calendar.

If Margaret was looking for a distraction, perhaps this would be the very thing. Charles watched as she set about arranging flowers and composing the guest list.

'Let's see. Meg and Fergus, obviously. I'll ask Randolph and Birdie Schwabe, and maybe they'll let Alice come as well, if they don't mind her staying up past her normal bedtime. I think Patrick and Anna Geddes are at home at the moment. Oh, and Rudolph Ihlee. What do you think?'

'Yes, of course,' said Charles. Rudolph was another artist that they had come to know through Meg's theatre club. 'And Eugene, I should imagine.'

'Why not? What about Harold Squires and his sister?'

'If you like,' said Charles. 'He's okay. Not sure about his sister.'

'Well, I'll ask them anyway.' She scribbled the names down, and Charles could tell she was already envisaging where the guests would sit – which arrangement would make for the most stimulating conversation.

* * *

The party was clearly a success, the Mackintoshes enjoying the healing power of their circle of friends. In the course of the evening, when speaking with Rudolph Ihlee, Charles turned again to the subject of how difficult it was proving to find lucrative work and the frustrations he was experiencing in dealing with the local authorities.

'Fergie thinks I should become a painter,' he said.

All conversation suddenly stopped as everyone around the table waited to hear if he was seriously considering this option.

'Well, why don't you?' said Meg.

Charles was slightly embarrassed to find the spotlight suddenly focussed on him and he shrugged his shoulders.

'There is the small matter of money,' he said. 'I have a wife to support.'

'Don't blame me,' said Margaret. 'I can live on practically nothing.'

'You just have to sell a few pictures,' said Fergusson.

Charles laughed. 'It's all very well for people like you and Ihlee. You're painting to order. Your names are known. I would have to establish a reputation. First things first.'

'I've decided I'm moving to the South of France,' said Rudolph. 'You might be surprised how cheap it is to live there. Do you know Edgar Hereford? He and I were at the Slade together, and we thought we might get a couple of rooms.'

'Have you decided where, exactly?'

'Yes. We have our eye on a little place called Collioure, close to the Spanish border. It has the greatest number of days of sunshine in France.'

'I've heard of it,' said Margaret. 'Isn't that where Matisse was living?'

'That's right. Matisse and Derain. The Fauvists. Matisse moved to Nice, but there's still quite a colony of artists in Collioure.'

'So, no competition, then,' said Charles, his tongue firmly in his cheek.

Rudolph held Charles's gaze to make sure he knew that what he was about to say was serious. 'I've seen your watercolours, Toshie. You don't need to worry about competition.'

*   *   *

In spite of their pipe dreams, life in Chelsea continued pretty much as before, and though Charles found the odd commission for textile designs, Margaret watched with mounting anxiety as their capital dwindled by the month. She began to toy with the idea that William Davidson might wish to purchase the flat at Florentine Terrace, and, when Charles agreed, William, true to form, came to their rescue again by taking it off their hands at the market price, giving them a little more under their belts to see them through the lean times.

With so little work on the horizon, they both had plenty of leisure. Meg called on them to assist with her next production – Charles with the scenery and Margaret with costumes. They were often to be found in the makeshift theatre, enjoying the work and the society of their friends.

One afternoon, Meg, arriving back from a visit to her solicitor, noticed Margaret sitting on her own towards the back of the auditorium, watching her husband paint the outlines of scenery on the flats in wild extravagant brush strokes. She went over to join her.

'You're very quiet today, Margaret.'

'Oh, hello, Meg. Yes, don't mind me. I'm feeling a bit low.'

'Tell me.'

Margaret turned and looked at her. Meg knew that Margaret could be intensely private, but she never gave up that easily.

'My mother,' said Margaret eventually. 'She passed away last night.'

'Oh, Margaret. I'm so sorry. Why didn't you say?'

'You know me...'

Meg took her hand. 'Yes, I do, so if you want to be on your own, just say, and I'll get on with something else.'

Margaret smiled. 'Well, it's not a huge shock, Meg. She's been unwell for a long time. But it's just...'

'I know.'

'... And, well, it sounds awful to say it, but there are now possibilities on the horizon.'

'You mean, you might go back to Glasgow?'

'No, no. My brother means to sell the house, which means we'll have some capital.' She remained quiet for a while, and Meg waited patiently until she said, 'What would you say if we were to move to France?'

'Oh, Margaret, that would be wonderful! You must!'

'Of course, Toshie and I would miss you and Fergus dreadfully...'

'And we'd miss you too. But you mustn't let that stop you. We'd come and see you, of course. I've been thinking I might try and run a summer school in Antibes. We'd practically be neighbours!'

'Don't say anything to Toshie. We haven't discussed it yet.'

'Do you think he'll agree?'

'Do you know, Meg, I think he'll jump at the chance.'

*   *   *

Somebody announced that tea had been made, so Charles put down his brush and everyone congregated at the front of the stage. Margaret threaded her way through the seats and picked up a cup and saucer. Randolph Schwabe appeared carrying a large tin of biscuits.

'Hello, Toshie,' said the professor. 'Keeping gainfully employed?'

'Just about, Schwabe, old man.'

'I thought you'd be working on the Arts League Studios...?'

'Pretty much dead in the water,' said Charles. 'I'm hoping Meg might be able to use that site.'

'Why, that would be excellent. Has she put in a bid?'

'A bid for what?' said Meg hearing her name mentioned.

'The site next to Harold Squire's studio,' said Randolph. 'I think it would be ideal for you.'

'I have my solicitor on it. There are so many conditions attached to that site, it's a bit of a nightmare.'

Having spotted the teapot, Fergusson had descended the ladder from the lighting rig and was wiping his hands on his overalls.

'How does Harold like his studio, Toshie? Did it turn out all right in the end?'

'Yes, he's very pleased. But...'

'There's a "but"?'

'He says it's haunted. There have been reports of a ghost rider that crosses the garden on his horse.'

'Yes, I heard something about that,' said Fergusson. 'Apparently the previous owner was rather eccentric, and rumour had it among the neighbours that he got up to all sorts of strange things. When they were excavating the site, they found the remains of an old church – pieces of carved stone, and what looked like remnants of an altar.'

'So, he might just have been very religious?' suggested Meg.

'Well, possibly. Except they also dug up the remains of a horse.'

Meg looked horrified. Fergusson, however, found the whole thing highly amusing.

'Harold can't keep any live-in staff,' said Randolph. 'They keep hearing the horse and handing in their notice.'

'And Harold has actually seen it, in broad daylight,' said Charles. 'Horse and rider. He had a medium come and investigate. She saw it too.'

Margaret placed her empty cup on the stage. 'Don't tell me Bertie's been up to his tricks again?'

'McNair...?' said Charles. What on earth do you mean? Bertie's been nowhere near Chelsea.'

There was a twinkle in her eye. 'As far as we know... Don't forget the White Lady.'

'I don't know what you're talking about,' said Charles. 'Are you all right, Margaret?'

She smiled. 'I'm fine, Toshie,' she said. 'Perhaps we just need a holiday.'

PART II

CHAPTER 8

MARGARET IS SLEEPING in the seat opposite Charles in their compartment. He watches as the trees by the side of the track cast intermittent shadows across her face and wonders how he could render in a painting the image flickering like a cinematic film caught in the projector gate. How, he wonders, could he convey that sense of movement, as opposed to a snapshot in a realistic style. He reflects that she is as beautiful as ever, reminding him of the idealised women painted by Rossetti and Burne-Jones. Perhaps she has become even more beautiful as her life and experiences have recorded their story around her eyes and mouth. Her tall stature gives her a presence that she uses to effect, often getting her own way with Charles, as well as with others that she wishes to influence. The white skin on her slender hands seems to have become almost transparent, and only tiny liver spots give any indication of her true years. Although her red hair is already tinged with touches of grey, it is still her crowning glory, and the colour benefits from the added undertone. He has painted her only once, and that too was in a non-realistic manner, in a portrait that he had called *Part Seen, Imagined Part*. Now, he seems to be looking at the imagined part.

She hasn't been in the best of health of late. Part of the attraction in heading south is to experience a kinder climate, since the perpetual damp of England seems to have wormed its way into Margaret's lungs. The hotel that they have been recommended in the South of France also promises the facilities of a spa.

As the train slows, the brakes screeching against the metal wheels, Margaret opens her eyes and yawns. 'Where are we?'

'Nearly at Narbonne,' says Charles. 'The oxter.'

She gives him one of her quizzical looks.

'Don't you know that good Scottish word, Margaret? The armpit. Also, part of a roof. You know, the rafters...' he placed his fingertips together, making a triangular arch with his hands. 'The ties are the horizontal members between the rafters, and the oxters are the vertical ones between the ties and the ceiling joists.'

Margaret smiles and nods. Charles now holds his left arm out at a right angle to his body, and runs the index finger of his right hand along its underside.

'Here, the Camargue, Montpellier and Béziers, where we are now.' He points to his armpit. 'Here, Narbonne.' Next he runs his finger down to the top of his ribcage. 'And there is Catalonia, Collioure, Port-Vendres, Cerbère.' Finally, he draws a line across his chest. 'The Spanish border.'

'And where is your heart?' Margaret asks, sleepily.

'I don't have a heart.'

'Don't be silly.' She reaches across and places a finger where his heart should be. 'Where is there?'

'Let me see, that would be Figueres, I think. That's where Salvador Dali's heart is.'

Margaret leans forward and moves her finger down to the middle of his belly. 'And there...?'

'Why, that must be Madrid!'

She sits back again and stretches. 'So... Narbonne.' As the train approaches the station, she sees signs of industry beginning to mar the landscape. 'Perpignan next. We must be nearly there.'

* * *

It has been a long journey. Yesterday morning they had taken the boat train to Dover, and crossed the channel to Boulogne before transferring their luggage on to the Paris express. A short taxi ride had taken them to the Gare du Lyon where they had boarded the night train to Perpignan. Since this leg of the journey would take over seventeen hours, they had elected to take a compartment in one of the Wagon Lits coaches. For reasons best known to the French Railway Company, they had to transfer into one of the ordinary coaches at Narbonne. Then it took another two hours for them to finally arrive at Perpignan.

There is time for a quick lunch in the station cafe. Enquiring what might be available to eat, they are told that the *croques madames* are renowned in the whole of France, but suspect that the cafe patron might be exaggerating. Nevertheless, they find that the cheese and ham sandwich topped with a fried egg fits the bill exactly, and with a glass of light beer to wash it down they feel sufficiently refreshed for the final leg of the journey.

The train to Amelie-les-Bains branches off the main line at Elne and meanders up the narrow valley, at times alongside the main road. Finally, it emerges in the tiny town that sits snugly into a fold of the mountains, where a warm sulphurous stream pours out of a lake and runs down along the edge of the main street.

The Hôtel Central proves easy to find. It is simple, but beautifully clean and very reasonably priced. As soon as the young porter has carried their luggage up to their room and handed them the key, Charles flops down on the bed.

'This is a lovely place,' he says, relaxing at last, while Margaret unpacks her dresses and hangs them in the wardrobe. 'I'm sure you will soon feel the benefit from the air and the waters.'

Margaret pauses in her labours and turns to smile at her husband. 'I think I'm feeling the benefit already.'

But they are both exhausted from the journey and, rather than exploring their new surroundings, they spend the rest of the day in bed.

* * *

They pass the next morning wandering around the little town and enjoy lunch in one of the cafes. Here, quite close to the border with Spain, they discover that the locals seem to be more Spanish than French, and it seems that all the local women are dressed in black. Most of them speak Catalan, although thankfully they understand French – another language that Margaret has a reasonable grasp of. After lunch, they take a short walk up to the spa at the top of the town, where Margaret has already reserved a course of treatment for her asthma. When she wrote to the spa from London regarding her therapy, she discovered that she could set up an arrangement to have their mail forwarded to the Hôtel Pujade which is attached to the baths, although it seemed that the hotel itself would be beyond their means as a place to stay.

Charles leaves her to it and walks back past the hotel to the bridge over the Tech. On the other side of the river, he begins a short exploration of the road that leads uphill away from the town, making a mental note of various opportunities to sketch or paint. He is looking forward to indulging in those very activities as soon as they are settled. But first, they need to find somewhere he can work indoors on his canvasses, their hotel room being too small for the purpose.

When Margaret rejoins Charles, she tells him that she asked in the spa if anyone knew of any such suitable accommodation, but most of the guests were tourists, and few of the staff were local. They decide instead to make enquiries at their own hotel, which proves to be much more fruitful. Just across the bridge there is an old toll house, owned by a Dr Bouix who lives in the house next door. The toll house has just two rooms, one on the ground floor, one upstairs, and suits their needs perfectly. Dr Bouix offers it to them at a price which, compared to what they were paying in London, seems almost laughably inexpensive.

The next day they set about installing themselves in their new studio. Charles wastes no time in getting his equipment ready. He has a little wooden box in which he arranges his brushes, pencils, a ruler and several lead tubes of water colour. In a corner he places an eraser. There is a tin palette on which he will mix his colours, and a tinting saucer for washes. He also finds a jar with a screw-on lid to carry fresh water when he's outdoors and a little canister to wash his brushes in. All of these he places in a small canvas haversack, which has space for some sandwiches if required. The greatest effort goes into preparing the boards, which are the equivalent of the canvasses that artists use for oil paint. He has acquired some sheets of millboard which are thick enough to resist bending, and on to each of these he pastes a sheet of lightly grained paper. He pins the corners to prevent them from curling up and then surveys his assembled equipment, wondering if he has forgotten anything; once he is out on the bluff, it will be too far to return to the hotel.

'You might need to buy an umbrella for some shade,' suggests Margaret.

'Too much to carry.'

'Then, what about a sunhat?'

'In January?'

'Yes, in January. You're not in Dunure now.'

Charles bows to his wife's sensible suggestion and stuffs a sunhat into the sandwiches' space. He can always come back down the hill when he's hungry.

'A walking stick?'

Charles slings his bag over his shoulder and picks up his boards with a shrug. 'No, I want to keep a hand free.'

'All set then?'

'All set.'

*   *   *

While Margaret continues with her treatment, Charles delves each day a little deeper into the mountain pass above the town until a bush of mimosa catches his interest. He relaxes into his well-practised method of drawing and painting that he perfected in Walberswick, knowing that, when they appraise his day's efforts back at the studio, Margaret will give him not only her valued opinion, but possibly a suggestion as to how the drawing could be improved. He will then sign his work with both their initials, as has been his habit.

But he is anxious to begin painting the landscape and his eye roves around in search of the ideal viewpoint, which could offer both scenery to his liking and a place for him to perch comfortably for as long as need be. In the neighbouring village of Palalda, he finds a jumble of little houses cascading down the hillside and makes two renditions of them, from a different viewpoint each time. Later, he decides to combine these into one picture by cutting along the outlines of the roofs of one of the paintings and pasting it over the lower part of the other. It is a masterstroke, because now the whole sense of the place is captured in one scene, the grey and white cottages contrasting with the symphony of greens that is the surrounding landscape.

Later in the week, he finds a little farmhouse further up the valley called Rui Bans. It nestles below a cliff, with a vantage point opposite that suits him ideally. Over a period of weeks, it becomes *Mont Alba*, a picture that perfectly conveys the sense of an oasis of agriculture in an otherwise barren and rocky landscape.

When the weather makes painting impractical, Charles seeks out some of the local vernacular architecture, fascinated as always by churches in particular. There is one such at the top end of Palalda, the church of Sant Martin which contains a magnificent rococo reredos. On his return, he tells Margaret how beautiful he thought it was.

'The wood isn't just carved. Somehow, they've resisted making it perfectly smooth, so you can see every mark of the tools they used. Then they don't just paint it, they clothe it in thick gold leaf. It is like a shrine, but not to religion. To art.'

On another occasion, he journeys to the neighbouring village of Prats-de-Mollo, and now finds himself at a loss for words to describe the stonework of the church there. The atmosphere is rather gloomy, but he puts the absence of daylight down to the fact that they were built for the congregation to listen to the priest, rather than reading the words of scripture.

And so the Mackintoshes begin to settle into this new environment, albeit with no intention of its becoming their permanent home. Not only does Margaret find the spa beneficial to her health, she also rejoices in the fact that, when she needs hot water, she can simply fill a can from the rivulet at the edge of the street. Despite its strong scent of sulphur, it is particularly good for washing her hair.

The location's micro-climate is very much to their liking, for though they are protected by the mountains from the Tramontane, the north-westerly wind, they find the strong breeze blowing off the snowy peak of Mont Canigou to the north-east exhilarating, as it imparts a sharpness to the sunlit days.

CHAPTER 9

ONE MORNING IN May, when Charles precedes Margaret down the stairs, the hotel proprietor tells him there's a letter waiting for him at the Hôtel Pujade. After breakfast, Charles collects it and takes it up to their room.

'It's from Ihlee,' he tells Margaret, as he takes the note from the envelope and carries it to the window to read. 'He wants us to join him for a while in Collioure. How would you feel about exchanging the mountain air for some ozone?'

Margaret is attracted by the idea of enjoying some sea air. She has felt so much better as a result of her treatment at the spa, and, since the weather has become warmer, feels it is probably time to move on.

'That would be wonderful,' she says. 'It will be lovely to see Rudolph again.'

Charles scribbles a reply to Ihlee, saying that they will come down to the coast at the end of the month. The hotel has a copy of the timetable for the local train, so he is able to tell their friend that they will arrive in Elne at half-past nine on the evening of the 30th. He imagines that there will be a connection to Collioure from there.

* * *

When they disembark at Elne, they are the only ones to do so, and find themselves on an almost deserted platform, looking out for a friendly porter. But before they can find one, a voice shouts, 'Charles! Margaret!' and they spot Rudolph Ihlee waving to them from outside the ticket office.

'Good heavens, Ihlee!' cries Charles. 'We were going to catch the next train to Collioure.'

'No need! Your carriage awaits.'

Margaret is delighted. 'This is so good of you, Rudolph. How are you? Are you well?'

They all embrace, the Mackintoshes happy to be reunited with a familiar face in these still foreign surroundings. Rudolph's car, an open-top tourer with two small seats in the back, is waiting for them in the station yard, its big brass headlamps creating a pool of light in front of it. Although the spring evening has already lost the warmth they enjoyed earlier in the day, they are excited by the prospect of a cooling breeze during the short drive to Collioure. The car journey exceeds their expectations: they are both awed by the rugged coastal scenery, and resist trying to converse above the combined noise of the wind and the engine.

They draw up outside the guest house where Rudolph and his friend Edgar Hereford have accommodation.

'I've managed to get a room for you here,' says Rudolph. 'Madame… I can never remember her surname… says you can have it till August if you want. I hope it'll be okay.'

'I'm sure it'll be perfect,' says Margaret. 'Thank you so much.'

Rudolph helps them carry their luggage up the stairs and shows them the room, which is across the landing from his own.

'Now, perhaps there's somewhere we can all go for a drink,' suggests Charles.

Rudolph doesn't need much persuading. 'There's a cafe that we use along the street. It's a bit different from the Blue Cockatoo, but it suits Edgar and me very well.'

A short walk takes them to the Café des Templiers, an unpretentious bar furnished with a selection of old mismatched tables and chairs, and the scent of Gauloises hanging heavy in the air. As they enter, the other occupants greet them with a 'Bon après-midi', and some of them raise their glasses. The three of them take a table near the bar.

'This is good,' says Charles, 'I like the atmosphere.'

The owner comes over brandishing his little notepad to take their order.

'Welcome to Des Templiers. I am Renée Pous.'

'Renée, these are my friends Mr and Mrs Mackintosh.'

'Are you also painters, like your friend?'

'No,' says Rudolph. 'Mrs Mackintosh paints, but Mr Mackintosh is an architect. He just thinks he can paint, as so many architects do.'

Charles shoots his friend a disdainful look and feels obliged to correct him. 'I've painted for years, Monsieur Pous, although I've only used watercolour. I need to learn how to paint in oils.'

'Well, I wish you good luck with that, Monsieur. How long do you intend to stay?'

Margaret explains that, at this point, they are unsure.

'*Eh bien,*' says Monsieur Pous. 'You must come here as often as you like. Any friends of Monsieur Ihlee are certainly friends of mine.'

They order glasses of the local wine and move over to a table by the windows that look out on to the dark street.

'I wonder if you might find it too hot here in the summer,' says Rudolph. 'If you use watercolour, you'll find the paint dries too quickly on the paper. I tend to wait till I'm back in the studio before I apply any colour.'

'All the more reason to move to oils,' suggests Charles.

Rudolph isn't so sure. 'Perhaps. Whatever you decide, you have to be comfortable in your chosen medium. Didn't you say you've been experimenting with landscape?'

Charles confirms that he had completed a couple of pictures whilst in Amelie.

'I would continue in watercolours, as you already have the technique. Then perhaps move on to oils later.'

Margaret smiles at him. 'We have all the time in the world, Rudolph. We can try everything.' Rudolph notes her use of 'we'. 'But when it's too hot here, where would you recommend?'

'Mont-Louis,' says Rudolph, without hesitation. 'You get the train back to Perpignan, then make a change for Ville-franche, where you can pick up the Petit Train Jaune – the narrow-gauge train that runs up the Têt valley. Or, come to that, if I'm around, I could run you to Villefranche.'

'Oh, we can't keep imposing on you, Rudolph.'

'Why not? It would be a pleasure.'

*   *   *

Charles's first undertaking in Collioure is a street scene in a style that is becoming his signature – a jumble of rooftops against a backdrop of upland farms – but he wants to expand his horizons, literally, without resorting to the overtly pictur-esque scenes that draw so many of the local artists. Finally, he finds a view that inspires him, with the town, backed by its fortress, seen across the bay. The panorama suggests a lay-ered treatment – bands of colour that depict rocks at the bot-tom of the picture, becoming the waves of the sea and finally the textures of the pan-tiled roofs. He feels as if he is manag-ing to develop a language in which to capture what he sees.

By the end of July, both Charles and Margaret find the temperature too extreme for them, and the atmosphere in their room is stifling. Despite Margaret's protestations, Rudolph Ihlee drives the Mackintoshes into the mountains towards Villefranche. As a compromise, they let him bring them only as far as the little town of Ille-sur-Têt, lower down in the Têt valley, where they could spend a few days before continuing their onward journey. They won't hear of detain-ing him while they look for accommodation, so he wishes them '*bonne chance*,' before roaring off out of the square in a cloud of exhaust fumes. It doesn't take long to discover a room in the Hôtel du Midi with a window overlooking the river valley. It is enchanting. The proprietor takes them up to the top floor, and leaves them to settle in.

After they have unpacked their things, Charles flings open the window and surveys the view with his elbows propped on the sill. Margaret comes up behind him and puts her arm over his shoulder.

'Do you think we could be happy here?'

He turns and smiles at her. 'There's no reason why we shouldn't be. It's like Walberswick with sunshine.'

'And without the sea.'

'Nae sea.'

She kisses him. 'We should be practising our French.'

'*Sans mer?*' he ventures.

'*C'est ça.*'

They spend a few days acclimatising. There are many opportunities to go for walks around the village, after which they can savour the relaxing environment of a street cafe where a glass of *vin ordinaire* costs less than a cup of tea in London. Sometimes they just stay on in the cafe and ask the proprietor what he has on his menu. There is usually something basic and wholesome to provide a more than satisfying dinner. More than that, however, they enjoy the atmosphere of a hotel that caters as much for the local workforce as for tourists like themselves. In a letter to Fergus back in London, Charles describes the scene in the dining room:

> At the end of the room there's a long table at which the workmen sit. There are usually between six and twelve splendid fellows sitting here discussing the affairs of the world. It somehow reminds me of the Last Supper, except there is no frugality here, and the wine flows in a way that would have given a little more life and gaiety to Leonardo's popular masterpiece.

By the end of the week, Charles begins to feel the call to move on – his wanderlust, as Margaret calls it. They make their way to the station where, following Rudolph Ihlee's recommendation, they buy two one-way tickets to Villefranche. Half an hour later, they disembark and transfer their belongings to the platform from where the Petit Train Jaune leaves for Mont-Louis.

When they are given permission to do so, they install themselves in one of the yellow-painted carriages, taking seats at either side of the window. The guard blows his whistle and the little train begins to snake up the valley, clinging to the steep side, with a precipitous drop to the river Têt below them. After climbing for almost two hours, the track suddenly swings out to the right, and begins to cross the valley on a slender suspension bridge, all but invisible to the passengers.

As the ground falls away and the views become ever more expansive, the couple are mesmerised. They begin to feel as if they are in an aircraft, and this sensation of flying is intensified as the train climbs into the higher reaches of the valley. When they finally disembark at the little station of Mont-Louis, although they are only in the foothills of the Pyrenees, it is as if they are on top of the world. Here, the air is dry and fresh, the light is clear and sharp, and they can see back down the whole of the Cerdagne valley. From the station it is one kilometre to the walled town where they hope to find a hotel and, as they carry their cases up the steep road, Charles has an overwhelming desire to stop and unpack his sketchpad and paints. But it can wait. Once they have discovered somewhere to lodge, they will explore their surroundings together. After that, he will probably take off on his own and record the local flora in watercolour – perhaps even try his hand again at landscape.

*　*　*

They are ecstatic at their choice of hotel, the Jambon providing them with the family atmosphere that they so relish along with an excellent service and standard of cuisine. After breakfast on their first day, they set off along one of the many pathways that radiate from the fortifications across the alpine meadows surrounding the village. The profusion of wild flowers along their route causes Margaret to remark that it is like fairyland.

'Hornel would love it,' says Charles. 'He would surround his be-smocked girls with all this flora and make us believe we could see fairies in the spaces between.'

'We should have brought our sketchbooks,' says Margaret.

'I suppose. But the weather is settled, my love, and we have endless days in which to indulge ourselves. Let's just take a day out to relax.'

As they come around to the east side of the hill, there is a view down the valley, and they can see the village of Fetges in the distance, its profusion of roof tops nestling in a crease of the landscape.

'Look,' says Charles. 'There's a picture waiting to be painted. If we can find a suitable rock for me to sit on, so that my bottom doesn't get too damp.'

'What you need,' says Margaret, 'is a little artist's stool, that you can fold up and tuck under your arm.'

'My easel under one arm,' says Charles, 'my boards and brushes under another. I can balance my colours on my head, and then I only need to conjure up one other arm for my stool. Perhaps I can get myself a cartie.'

The memory of street urchins careering down the Glasgow drumlins in their orange boxes mounted on a set of pram wheels makes Margaret laugh. 'You'll find a way.'

* * *

An hour later they are back at the hotel. As they wait at the desk for the clerk to give them the key to their room, the proprietor appears carrying a sheaf of mail.

'Monsieur Mackintosh, I have a telegram for you.'

Excited and curious, Charles tears open the envelope. It is from Meg, and reads, 'Summer school Antibes. Stop. Getting funding together. Stop. Hope you can contribute. Stop.'

He shows the telegram to Margaret. 'We shall have to phone her. How can she possibly imagine that we can afford to make a contribution?'

They decide to wait for the evening, when there will be a greater chance of getting Meg at home. In the meantime, they retire to their room and Charles makes plans for the equipment he will need for his painting.

Later, Charles asks the hotel clerk to try and put a call through to Meg. A short while afterwards the clerk hands Charles the instrument, looping the cable out across the reception desk.

'Meg,' he shouts. 'How did you know where to find us?'

'I contacted Rudolph,' she says. The line is crackly and she sounds a long way off. 'He told me where you were.'

'Your summer school,' says Charles. 'That sounds very exciting, but please, you must realise that Margaret and I have very little money.'

'That's all right,' says Meg. 'The school will pay for your accommodation.'

'But you were looking for a contribution.'

Despite the bad connection, Meg's tinkling laugh sounds clear across the miles. 'Not money, Toshie. I want you to contribute to the proceedings. I'm looking for a guest speaker.'

Suddenly Charles understands, and begins to feel the fire of enthusiasm ignite somewhere in his belly. 'But that would be wonderful, Meg. Of course we'll come.' They spend a few more minutes as Meg gives him the briefest of details about her proposal. Then, passing the phone back across the reception counter, Charles goes to find Margaret. He knows she will be equally excited.

'August in Antibes,' he says. 'We can take the train from Perpignan.'

Margaret nods. 'How nice it will be to have Meg and Fergus's company here in France.'

'Fergie can show me his plantain.'

'Fergus will also show you the bar from where he spotted his plantain.'

'And introduce me to the delights of absinthe, no doubt.'

'No doubt,' agrees Margaret, not bothering to disguise her disapproval.

With a spring in his step, Charles returns to their room to fetch his sketchbook, picks up his pipe and tobacco pouch, and strolls out to the garden to take advantage of the last rays of sunshine in the cool mountain air.

* * *

The hotel room allocated for the lecture is light and airy, which is just as well, as every seat is occupied and there's an expectant buzz. When Charles enters, a sudden hush ensues. He has no need to call the house to order.

His audience listens respectfully as he introduces himself. He suspects that none of them really know who he is, despite the notes that Meg has thoughtfully provided on the programme of events. They are, after all, students of dance, not architecture. Nevertheless, as he warms to his subject, he senses that he has their attention; there are no signs of fidgeting, yawning, or stray glances through the festooned windows to the sparkling waters of the Mediterranean visible beyond the terrace. After he draws his talk to a close, he asks if there are any questions. Hands shoot up around the room, one of them belonging to a young lady with a shock of red hair, reminding Charles vividly of Margaret when she was younger.

'Yes...?' he says. 'Lady in the fourth row. What is your question?'

'Good afternoon, Mr Mackintosh. My name is Charlotte Reilly. I have seen one of your drawings of a house that you designed in a magazine. My friend thought it was lovely, but I'm afraid I couldn't make anything of it.' There is a subdued gasp from some members of the audience and Charles gives her a slightly bemused look. 'My question is: if I were to see the actual building, do you think I would like it any better?'

'Thank you for your question, Miss Reilly. You have to remember that a drawing is only lines on a page. You have to look between the lines. What house was it that you saw?'

'I think it was called "The House of an Artist," or something like that.'

'Ah, the *House for an Art Lover* was never built, so you would not be able to see it, even if you wanted to. But I suspect that, even if you could, if you didn't like the drawing, you wouldn't like the building any better.'

He sees another hand go up.

'The young lady at the back.'

The young lady rises to her feet. Even in that brief manoeuvre, he can tell that she has the poise of a dancer.

'Mr Mackintosh.' In those two words, Charles detects an American accent. 'Do you think the way you assess a work of architecture has anything in common with the way you would assess dance?'

'It's a good question, Miss...?'

'Duncan,' says the questioner as she resumes her seat.

'Well, Miss Duncan. My mentor, Francis Newbery, used to say that the education of all artists must be conducted on one grand principle, and therefore they must all be educated alike – with one common aim. Is this possible, do you think? Can you educate dancers the same way that you educate painters?'

There is a murmur among the audience, until they realise it was a rhetorical question.

'Let's think about this. Is there a common standard we are aiming for, and, if there is, how are we to judge whether we have achieved it? When it comes to beauty, there is no final standard of taste to which we could all refer, no code of laws to which every little detail may be submitted – no authoritative committee of tastes to decide on disputed points. The faculty of distinguishing good from bad in art is a faculty which most educated people – and especially ladies – believe they possess, although few would be able to explain how it has actually been acquired. The general impression seems to be that it is the peculiar inheritance of gentle blood, and independent of all training. But we know better, don't we?'

There is a ripple of amusement. He has drawn in his audience as if they are members of a shared conspiracy.

'We have to clothe modern ideas in modern dress – adorn our designs with living fancy. The message will still be of nature and mankind, of order and beauty. The new, the future, is to aid life and train it so that beauty may flow into the soul like a breeze. Every age has its own spirit to express, its own truth to tell, and no trammels of set opinion or fixed standards of beauty should ever be allowed to fetter the freedom of an artist to express him or herself. So, in the end, if you were to ask how you are to judge dance, the answer is just as you would judge painting or sculpture or architecture – form, colour, proportion, all visible qualities – and the one great invisible quality in all art, soul.'

Miss Duncan seems to be satisfied with the answer.

'Now, then. Are there any more questions?'

Charles spots another young lady with her hand raised sitting in the second row.

'Yes...?'

'Mr Mackintosh. You draw comparisons between all branches of the arts, so I think you would agree that, like dance, in architecture it is impossible to cover up your mistakes. My question is: do any of your buildings contain what you would consider mistakes – things which, with hindsight, you would have designed differently?'

'Thank you, Miss...?'

'Wilson.'

'Thank you for your question, Miss Wilson. My answer is yes. All of them.'

There is a murmur of amusement around the room.

'You see, every building project, like every dance project, is an experiment. We learn all the time, and we make mistakes all the time. We are all human beings, and no human is perfect. Therefore, no building can be perfect, and no dance can be perfect. Someone once said to me "doctors are lucky, because they can bury their mistakes". But doctors are not artists. We are artists, and of course we make mistakes.'

Lifting his glass of water from the table, he takes a sip.

'However, don't be discouraged, Miss Wilson. There is hope in honest error...'

And before he can finish his sentence, the entire audience chimes in with, '... None in the icy perfections of the mere stylist.'

There is a round of applause and when it stops, Charles, aware of an incipient lump in his throat, comments, 'Clearly you have all done your homework. I'm very touched. Thank you for your attention. You have been a marvellous audience.'

A further round of applause serves as a reciprocal vote of thanks.

The room empties and Fergusson appears at the door, waving to Charles in a clear invitation to join him for a drink. As they make their way through to the hotel bar, Fergusson asks Charles how his lecture was received.

'I think it went very well,' says Charles. 'It's such a privilege to talk to a young audience. The impression that they are hanging on your every word is quite gratifying. It does feel as if you are actually having some sort of influence.'

Fergusson slaps him on the shoulder. 'Don't worry about it, Toshie. They'll have forgotten everything you said by the morning.'

After getting themselves ensconced in a couple of club chairs on the terrace, Fergusson spots the barman collecting glasses, and signals to him to take their order.

'This splendid fellow is Pablo,' says Fergusson, and turning to him requests two glasses of his best Cabernet Sauvignon.

'*Enchanté*, Pablo,' says Charles, which Pablo acknowledges with a slight inclination of his head.

Charles asks Fergusson how Meg thinks the event is going.

'I think she's very pleased,' says his friend. He lowers his voice as if he is about to impart a confidence. 'It's probably been a greater success than she imagined. She's already talking about doing it again next year. I assume you would have no objection to a repeat performance.'

'I can think of nothing I'd like better,' says Charles.

'Good,' says Fergusson. 'Perhaps we can make a holiday of it.'

Charles laughs. 'I feel as if I'm permanently on holiday. It's almost too good to be true. I half expect to wake up at any moment and find myself back in the office of Honeyman and Keppie.'

'But, are you finding enough to occupy your time?'

'Almost. But I have a strange sense of inertia. Margaret organises me, bless her, and saves me from slipping into a complete state of sloth. I don't know what I would do without her.'

'We need our ladies,' says Fergusson. 'It would be nice to think they need us as much as we need them, but I'm not sure whether that is the case.'

Charles ponders that one for a moment. Then he says, 'I think Margaret needs me to need her.'

Fergusson grins at him. 'You think too much, my friend. You and Margaret, like Meg and I, are there to help each other. Mark my words, when the time comes, she will need you, and you will be there for her, every inch of the way.'

At that moment, he spots Margaret entering the room with Meg.

'Ah. Talk of the devil!' He beckons them over. 'We're having a drink, Margaret. Will you join us? Meg?'

'Later, Fergus,' says Meg. 'Toshie, I want you to come and meet Pablo.'

'I've already met him,' says Charles, holding his wine glass aloft.

Meg looks confused for a moment, and then laughs. 'Not that Pablo. Pablo Picasso. He's in the next room.'

Rendered practically speechless, Charles rises from his seat and takes Margaret's hand, before allowing Meg to lead them out of the room, as if they have just been invited to an audience with the Pope.

CHAPTER 10

WHEN CHARLES AND Margaret return to the Roussillon, they
decide to look for a hotel a little further down the coast at
Port-Vendres. Not far from the station, they find a tall building on a street corner fronting the quay, the Hôtel du Commerce. Dragging their luggage inside, they look around the
salon and feel immediately drawn to the homely atmosphere.
A friendly voice says, 'Can I 'elp you M'sieur?'

Margaret takes over as usual, with the benefit of her
command of the language, and in no time has established a
mutually agreeable rate at which they can rent a room each
on the first floor for an indefinite length of time.

'When it becomes too hot for us here, Monsieur,' she
explains, 'we shall retreat to the mountains.'

'At Amelie-les-Bains?'

'*Oui*, possibly. Or Mont-Louis. We like the Hôtel Jambon very much.'

'I hope you will like it here, also. My name is Renée
Déjean, and this...' he gestures towards the woman wiping
the tables in front of the bar, 'this is my wife.'

'*Enchantée Monsieur, Madame*,' says Margaret.

Monsieur Déjean summons a waiter, who carries first
Margaret's luggage upstairs and then returns for Charles's.
Two rooms await them, their doors on opposite sides of the
landing, each with a little fireplace, which will come into
its own in the winter months. Charles makes an approving
appraisal of the rooms, before lighting his pipe and returning
to the street where he casts his eye over the scene from the
edge of the quay.

As soon as Margaret joins him, he says, 'I think this
will suit us very well. I like the topography of this place.

There should be a number of different places where I can try my hand at landscape.'

Their first priority is to explore and so, after a light lunch with a glass of wine, they set off together around the harbour along a route that takes them out of the environs of the busy port. Now the road follows the rocky coast, and twice plunges into tunnels below the headland for a reasonably short distance on each occasion. Thus, they are never completely in the dark and can be easily spotted by any approaching vehicles.

Beyond the tunnels they can see the lighthouse on the end of the harbour wall, reaching far out into the bay. Charles surveys the panorama before him and takes in the way the terraced buildings of the town are reflected in the still waters of the bay.

'The light is amazing, isn't it, Margaret? Look at the landscape over there. It's like a patchwork quilt.'

Margaret puts her hand on his shoulder to steady herself and looks at what he is looking at, seeing what he sees. 'You will transform that landscape. I know you will.'

'Help ma Boab, Margaret. You make me sound like a developer!'

She laughs, but inside she feels enormous excitement at the prospect of Toshie embracing his new life as a painter.

*   *   *

When they arrive back at the hotel, they are surprised to see Rudolph Ihlee sitting in the bar with his friend Edgar Hereford.

'Ihlee!' cries Charles. 'I didn't see your car outside?'

'That's because it isn't there! Margaret, how are you?'

Rudolph embraces her, kissing her on both cheeks, before vigorously shaking Charles's hand.

'We've just come off the train,' explains Edgar. 'It didn't stop in Collioure. Both our cars are in Perpignan, getting repaired.'

'Don't tell me you managed to collide with each other?' asks Margaret, who, having witnessed at least one of them drive, feels that this might be entirely possible.'

'Well, not quite,' says Rudolph. 'Can I get you some drinks before I regale you with all the details?'

Returning from the bar, he embarks on his tale of woe. He and Edgar were driving back from Perpignan a week ago where they'd been partying with some friends.

'It must have been about four o'clock in the morning,' says Rudolph, 'so it still wasn't light. I rounded a bend, and the next thing I knew, I'd run into the back of a cart piled high with strawberries.'

Charles winks at Margaret, suspecting that their friend may not have been entirely sober by the time he headed for home.

'It was practically stationary,' Rudolph continues, 'blocking the whole carriageway. I mean it's the last thing you expect to come across at that time in the morning.' He pauses, knocking back his drink. 'Well this *paysan* made quite a fuss, I can tell you. I mean, there was no damage to his cart at all, and compared with the load he had, the loss of a few strawberries over my car amounted to next to nothing. But the only way I could get rid of the fellow was to pay him off. I tell you Toshie, when I opened my wallet, he had such a greedy look on his face, as if I was unwrapping a parcel of sandwiches and he hadn't eaten for a week.'

'So, what was the damage to your car?' Charles wants to know.

'Well the front mudguard was broken, and the paintwork scraped off all down one side. But the worst of it was that the damned strawberries had got into every last nook and cranny of the vehicle, including the gearbox and steering gear. All the way back to Collioure, my car was behaving like some industrialised jam-making machine.'

'Perhaps you could have recovered the compensation you had to pay him by selling the jam,' suggests Margaret, with a twinkle in her eye.

Rudolph gives her a rueful smile. 'Perhaps I should have claimed compensation from him for the cost of getting all the fruit out of the inside of my car. The entire engine and gearbox had to be stripped out and overhauled.'

It seems to Margaret that this was hardly the poor peasant's fault, but she makes no comment.

'And your car, Hereford?' asks Charles. 'What happened to it?'

'Oh, mine had been needing a new hood for ages. When Rudolph found a garage that would do his, I just thought I'd get mine done at the same time.'

Charles and Margaret exchange glances. It occurs to them both that it might have been more sensible to leave Edgar's car until Rudolph's was fixed, so that they would at least have the use of one car between them. Perhaps there is something else that they aren't being told.

'So, that was our story,' says Rudolph. 'What are your plans now?'

'Our plans are to paint,' says Charles.

The two boys look at Margaret. Somehow it had not dawned on them that Margaret might also be intending to paint here in Collioure. Is Charles using the royal 'we', they wonder.

She reads the question in their eyes. 'When Toshie says "we", he's referring to the fact that he doesn't really function without me.'

They look at Charles, fully expecting him to deny this; but instead he is beaming at his wife and nodding in agreement. 'We operate as a unit, my Margaret and I. She advises, cajoles, encourages. How do you think I got this far?'

* * *

The next day, Charles and Margaret leave the hotel after breakfast and wander through the town together. There is much activity in the harbour where Charles is mesmerised by the various boats and their cargoes.

'Look at this one, Margaret, the *Acola*. It looks like they're carrying some sort of bean.'

Margaret follows his gaze. 'I think they're carob pods,' she says. 'They use the beans medicinally, and I seem to remember hearing that they're considered a healthy substitute for chocolate.'

'That's a weird noise it's making. Ker-phutter, ker-phutter. It sounds like your sewing machine.' He continues a little way along the edge of the dock. 'And this one. The *Esperos*. Surely that can't be gold dust?'

'Sulphur, by the smell of it.'

Two of the crew are having a heated discussion in a language they don't recognise.

'Isn't it strange,' says Margaret, 'how you get an ear for French, and then you just know when something you overhear isn't French? They must be speaking Catalan, surely?'

Charles isn't so sure. 'I've heard some pretty strange French here. That lad in the tobacconist. I could hardly make out a word he was saying.'

'Nor I. But remember I frequently had difficulty understanding some of the boys in Dennistoun.'

'Ah, Dennistoun. Doesn't that seem like an age away? When I was at school there and we heard about the Wild West, I used to think they meant Glasgow, but it's more likely the Glaswegians thought of Dennistoun as the Wild East.'

They continue around the port until they come to the heart of the town, and then head up a bluff from where they expect to obtain a new view out over the Mediterranean. There appears to be an old fort on its summit, and Charles quickens his step as he realises it's a possible subject for him to paint. The air is bracing here, the wind coming up off the sea.

'You might have to wait for the wind to drop,' says Margaret.

'I'm sure there'll be calmer days. I've a feeling Monsieur Déjean will have a handle on the weather. I'll ask him what it's going to be like tomorrow.'

Margaret settles on a rocky outcrop while Charles makes the circuit of the fort. When he returns, his excitement is palpable. 'What a wonderful edifice! It must be Moorish. It practically grows out of the terrain. Its strength is in its cliff-like structure.'

'I'm sure you can express that in paint.'

'I'll have a go.'

He makes another perambulation, stopping frequently to consider the best aspect, and looking for a suitable location where he can perch with his paints and brushes.

'This is going to be a good start,' he declares, as he rejoins Margaret at the seat which nature has provided for her. He puts his arm around her shoulder. 'What will you do while I'm painting?'

'Oh, don't worry about me. I'll walk, or I'll read, I'll do some sewing, or I'll write to Meg, or to Jessie Newbery, or to Anna Geddes.' She takes a deep lungful of sea air. 'If I have a worry, it's whether I'll have enough time to do all the things I want to do.'

* * *

The wind has dropped. Perched on a rock in front of the Moorish Fort, Charles feels exhilarated by the freedom of his isolation. Just him and his subject and the light breeze from the ocean. Except for the solitary crow who wheels overhead and then alights on the rocks opposite as if curious to know what Charles is up to.

'Good afternoon, Mr Crow,' he says, squeezing green paint from one of the tubes onto his palette. Later, a large

Dalmatian comes sniffing around, and Charles recognises it as belonging to the proprietor of the Café des Templiers in Collioure.

'Hello, fellow. You're a long way from home.' He glances around, expecting to see Monsieur Pous toiling up the hill, but there is no sign. The dog comes up to Charles, sniffs his knee, and then licks his hand, clearly remembering him from their short stay in May.

'When you go back to Collioure,' says Charles, wondering if he should be speaking French, 'give your owner my regards and tell him that I hope to see him soon.'

The dog gives a single bark, and sets off back down the hill, causing Charles to wonder at the animal's apparent comprehension.

Back at the hotel, he tells Margaret about his encounter.

'Well, it's nice that you had some company.'

'And you?'

'I've had a lovely afternoon with Rosa. She is fascinated by Scotland and says she would like to visit. She wanted to know if they speak English there, because she's trying to learn it. I told her that it's a kind of English.'

'Did you teach her to say, "It's a braw bricht moonlicht nicht"?'

'I told her that you say "drookit" instead of "drowned", and it's a word you'll need because it rains constantly.'

Charles laughs. 'I think Rosa will look after you very well. Monsieur Déjean has very loyal staff: Rosa for you and Kim for me.'

'I'm not sure that Kim aspires to being a valet.'

'No, but he does want to learn English.'

Margaret gives him one of her old-fashioned looks. 'Be careful what you teach him.'

'I shall be the soul of discretion,' says Charles.

* * *

Kim isn't Charles's only pupil. When walking out through the town a few days later, a boy of about ten years of age falls into step with him and asks where he is going. Charles has to get to him to repeat the question a few times before he can make out the child's accent.

'*Puis-je vous accompagner?*'

'*Pourquoi?*'

After a great deal of repetition and gesticulation, Charles realises that the boy wants to learn to paint. He is unsure how to respond; part of him is flattered, but he values his solitude and his privacy. He finally manages to convey that the boy will have to ask his parents, whereupon he scampers off, apparently satisified.

'He reminded me of Billy English in Walberswick,' Charles tells Margaret later, as he cleans his palette in the bathroom at the end of the corridor. 'But I don't know if he'll be such a good pupil. Anyway, he might not turn up tomorrow.' He wipes the palette dry with pages from an old *Observer*. 'Tell you something, though. As far as our league of strange accents is concerned, he must be pretty well at the top.'

Returning to his room, he fetches the boards which he brought back from his walk, sandwiched together so that the surface he had been working on was protected from damage, and separates them to show Margaret.

'What do you think?'

Margaret places her hand on his shoulder and casts her well-practised eye over his work. 'It's very green,' she says.

'Too much, do you think?'

She nods. 'I think it detracts from the solidity of the fort, makes it look too pastoral.'

'I agree,' says Charles. 'I don't know why I do it. The tube of paint is always the first one I go for. I shall have to rid myself of the habit. Tomorrow, I'll try it with a little less.'

* * *

The next day, Charles's little pupil is waiting for him at the same spot. Together they make their way up to the fort, and Charles gives the boy his sketchpad to work on and one of his pencils. But it is clear almost immediately that he has no natural talent, and he bombards Charles with questions which, for the most part, mean nothing to him. He is nothing but a distraction, and Charles is rather pleased when, the following day, he is nowhere to be seen.

CHAPTER II

'I TOLD YOU that you wouldn't like it.'

Margaret screws up her face and pushes the *demi-tasse* of espresso towards her husband across the little three-legged table.

'You told me I wouldn't like Italy.'

'Well...?'

'Well, I do like Italy, and, if you are to be honest, so do you.'

Charles opens his mouth to speak but Margaret cuts across him. 'You have some snobbish imperative to find fault, and whilst there are undoubtedly faults to be found, so there are in the buildings of any city in Europe, Glasgow included.'

Charles smiles. 'We have to find fault in order to counterbalance the weight of opinion from all those people who believe that anything and everything that comes out of Italy, or exists in Italy, has to be, per se, perfect.'

It is Margaret's turn to smile. 'Even the coffee...?'

'Even the coffee.'

After their three years in France, Charles has reluctantly agreed to take Margaret to see Italy. When he visited the country as a student, he had failed to be impressed by much of what he saw. But it is never a hardship to indulge his wife, and her presence will hopefully give him a new perspective, through her eyes. In their first week, they visited Genoa and Portofino. Finally arriving in Florence, they have found a small *pension* near the River Arno and, as their room receives its daylight from an internal courtyard, they have been unable to resist making frequent references to Forster's famous novel. Charles mischievously suggested that if Margaret were to flutter her eyelids at a certain Mr Emerson – this, of course, not his real name – who has been sitting at the table behind theirs at dinner, then he would probably agree to change rooms with them, because after all, a view would hold no appeal for a gentleman, whereas for a lady like herself the outlook is everything. And Margaret duly protested that she could not possibly allow them to be beholden to such a man. Then, on the arrival of a young lady with her chaperone, they instantly christened her Miss Honeychurch, and had the greatest difficulty keeping their faces straight at breakfast when they couldn't help overhearing part of their conversation.

Margaret nudged Charles and whispered, 'Did you hear that?'

'I don't believe it! Her name's Lucy!'

'It's not possible! If her friend happens to be called Charlotte, I'll think I've fallen asleep and woken up inside the novel!'

* * *

They have passed an agreeable morning in the Uffizi Palace, Charles regaling Margaret with the way he reacted to what he saw when he came here before. When he first entered what he calls 'this world of refinement', he had felt that he could have taken up residence in it for ever.

'I didn't know where to start,' he told her, 'and I ran around the endless array of sculptures, like a butterfly in the garden, skimming over ten thousand blooms before choosing the one to alight on.'

Margaret shared her husband's enthusiasm for the masterpieces of bronze and marble, and as they paused under the bust of *Jupiter Olympus* in order to appreciate the features of the *Minerva*, Charles said to her, 'Doesn't she just breathe divinity?'

'This from a man who has no time for religion,' said Margaret, but she knew what he meant. Like him, she was spellbound by the *Venus de Medici*, the warm ivory hue of the original marble and the softness of the limbs exhibiting a beauty that could never be surpassed or imitated, even though it was itself a copy.

Now they are sitting outside a bar in the Piazza della Signoria enjoying the afternoon sunshine. Behind them stands the replica of Michelangelo's *David*, uncompromisingly guarding the door of the Palazzo Vecchio, though clearly not expecting too much trouble since he's naked and, apart from his sling, unarmed. They cannot quite decide whether to join the considerable queue to see the real thing, or to climb out of the city and admire the view back over it from the Boboli Gardens. Suddenly, a man in a white linen jacket and a straw boater stops in front of their table.

'It's Mr and Mrs Mackintosh, isn't it?'

For a moment neither can think who this man is, or how he can have recognised them. Then they realise it's none other than their Mr Emerson from the *pension*.

'Please join us,' says Margaret.

'I'm going to order a tea, although God only knows what it will be like,' he says, pulling a chair up to their table. 'Can I get you anything?'

Charles shakes his head. 'No, thank you. We're going to move on after this. I think we might go and see the Boboli Gardens.'

'Oh, highly recommended!' exclaims their friend. 'I was there yesterday. It's something of a relief from looking at buildings. I mean, you can only take so much architecture, don't you think?' He looks at each of them for their agreement, and seeing Charles's slightly bemused expression, recalls with embarrassment what his profession is.

'Oh, but – of course – you're an architect! You must be revelling in all of it.'

'Even an architect needs a holiday from buildings,' says Margaret. 'And, with Charles's training, he can be a little hyper-critical at times.'

Charles is trying not to be drawn into an argument.

'But the Duomo is exquisite, isn't it?' says Mr Emerson.

It is too much to resist. 'Brunelleschi's dome is magnificent,' Charles agrees. 'As to the rest... Well...'

Margaret intervenes again. 'The Italian style is somewhat different from our home-grown architecture. Charles finds it hard to swallow.'

'Tell me,' says Mr Emerson. 'I'm interested.'

'The architecture that I understand,' says Charles, 'is of a piece. The inside reflects the outside and vice versa. Here when you enter a cathedral, you find something entirely different from what the exterior led you to expect. To me it seems... well, dishonest. The interior of the Duomo depends entirely for effect on the quality of the materials used and the variegated colours of the marble.' He looks at Margaret to see if she thinks he's saying too much, but her expression gives nothing away. 'Mind you, I'm talking purely in architectural terms here. I grant you that there is a striking effect achieved by the yellowy-greenish light which filters down through the narrow windows high up in the dome. Somehow it manages to suggest sanctity and makes me feel by contrast rather profane.'

'Ah, I see what you mean. Perhaps you have been to Siena? The cathedral there surely would not disappoint you.'

Margaret prepares herself for a lecture. Perhaps they should have accepted their friend's offer of further refreshment.

'We haven't been to Siena on this trip,' says Charles. 'But I have visited the cathedral there previously, and I'm afraid I found it even more of a fraud than this one.' He stretches back in his chair as he warms to his subject. 'When you examine the west front, it's a very poor composition, with some rather clumsy details. The interior of the front door is so clumsy it's practically ugly. And did you not notice the windows? There are none in the aisles, but the Italians love their windows, so if you look outside you find they are just painted on. Did you ever hear of such a thing? You could hardly imagine a worse sham. They are actually very nicely executed in the Gothic style, but the rain is wearing some parts of them away. And those bands of coloured marble, well, they must either have run out of the material or the funds to buy it, because at the upper levels of the interior, they're also just painted on. As for the dome, I couldn't see anything beautiful about it, either inside or out. It's very badly designed.'

'Did you not find any part of it that pleased you?'

Charles pauses to knock the remnants out of his pipe and pack some fresh tobacco into it. 'Actually, the floor. It's really magnificent, but a lot of it is covered up, so you don't get to see if properly, although you can see drawings of the whole thing in the Opera del Duomo. The tiling incorporates scenes from the Bible, most exquisitely designed, especially the one of Moses striking the rock. And there are fragments of ancient *sgraffito* work in there that would make you hair stand on end: figures delineated only by means of a shadow effect on a cream or ivory marble background with shadows in a pale green plaster. Quite amazing.'

'Forgive me. *Sgraffito*?'

'It's where the paint is applied in layers,' Charles explains, 'and then you scrape off parts of one layer to reveal the colour underneath.'

'I see. I shall have to go back and have another look. But what about the bell tower? Did you not find that impressive?'

'Ah, now, the *campanile* is good. Its virtue is its simplicity – square and plain, instead of all fussy and excited like the cathedral. I like the fact that it is completely solid at the lowest floor levels, and then gets one opening on the second floor, and then one more on each successive storey until you get six at the top. So the top of the tower is lighter than the bottom, which gives it balance, you see? Not top-heavy at all. It's just a pity they couldn't have made a better job of the main roof, which has been brought to a point in the most unseemly manner conceivable, and just as clumsy as those on the front turrets.' He swings round to point at the tower adjacent to the Palazzo Vecchio behind them – 'You know, that tower there is just a crib of the *campanile* at Siena, only without the horizontal bands or the openings.'

'No, I didn't. But, of course. Now you come to mention it…'

'You'll be sorry you mentioned Siena, Mr…' Margaret nearly calls him 'Mr Emerson'.

'Nichol,' says Mr Emerson, and drains his coffee cup. 'Not at all. It's been a most interesting insight.'

Taking their leave of Mr Nichol, Charles and Margaret walk back to the River Arno and cross the Ponte Vecchio.

'Isn't this a great bridge?' remarks Charles, trying not to be distracted by the stalls that line the thoroughfare.

'I love these bridges that have buildings on them,' agrees Margaret. 'Imagine living on a bridge! I think London Bridge was like this and there's one in Bath. In fact, there are examples all over Europe, aren't there?'

'The Rialto in Venice,' says Charles. 'Why didn't we build bridges like this in Glasgow?'

They climb the steep road up to the Boboli Gardens, both struggling with the severity of the incline in the heat. After passing through the museum, they emerge in the gardens and gaze over the manicured geometries.

Margaret can already tell what Charles is thinking.

'It's a bit…' he begins.

'Formal?'

'It's stuck, isn't it? Shouldn't gardens be allowed to… grow?'

'It's of its time.'

'But need it be? I don't know. We should ask Patrick.'

The previous year they had visited the Geddeses in Montpellier where Patrick had finally achieved his ambition of founding a Scots College as an international teaching establishment. In designing the buildings, he had recreated a lookout tower echoing the one that housed the Camera Obscura in Edinburgh; but what had most impressed the Mackintoshes were the terraced gardens – the *parterres* – conceived as a place of learning since Patrick preferred to teach outdoors whenever possible. If Charles had thought them too formal, then he must have bitten his tongue.

'*Il faut cultiver notre jardin*,' says Charles. 'Isn't that what Patrick said?'

'Voltaire,' Margaret corrects him.

'Who?'

'Voltaire. That's a quote from *Candide*. But it's not really to do with gardening. It's a metaphor for life.'

'Well, anyway. Patrick obviously agreed with Voltaire. This is stagnant.'

They arrive at the edge of the terrace from where they overlook the bowl of the city: a higgledy-piggledy roofscape of terracotta pantiles with the great dome of the Duomo rising from its centre and surrounded by a hazy ring of blue mountains.

'Now, there's a view,' says Charles.

'You can't fault it from here,' agrees Margaret. 'Who was it said, "Like the waterlily rising on the mirror of the lake, so rests on this lovely ground the still more lovely Florence"?'

'Well, that wasn't your Voltaire,' says Charles. 'I think it might have been Ruskin. Well remembered, Margaret.' He lights his pipe, puffs on it for a moment and then says, 'But don't you feel sometimes that it's all a little bit too perfect?'

'In what way?'

'It's as if the whole city has been designed for us, the tourists, rather than to assist the ebb and flow of the city's own lifeblood. Where are the traders, the artisans and the craftspeople?'

'Perhaps you're right. Perhaps we are in a giant museum. The real city is elsewhere. Do you want us to go and find it?'

'No, because if it is separate, as we think it is, it will hold no attraction for us.'

'But if it were integrated, as you think it should be, you would criticise it on the same basis that you criticised Rome.'

'What was that?'

'Let me remind you. You said that Rome bore a very striking resemblance to some parts of the east end of Glasgow – assuming about two-thirds of the population were dead of cholera. That it was as grimy, as filthy, as tumblesome and as forlorn, and unpleasantly redolent of old clothes and old women who were once washerwomen and had long foresworn soap'

'You have an extraordinary memory, Margaret. I may have said something like that.'

'So, you didn't like Rome?'

'Not especially.'

'But you would prefer Florence to be a bit more like Rome?'

'You're putting words in my mouth. I would simply prefer it if Florence were a little less...'

'Artificial?'

'Perhaps.'

* * *

When they return to their *pension*, the proprietor's twenty-year-old son is in the lobby, in command of the reception desk. Charles asks for the key to room number *ventiquattro*, and Emilio compliments him on his Italian.

'I like to have a go,' says Charles, secretly pleased.

'So... what else have you learned?' asks Emilio.

His bluff called, Charles has to admit that he hasn't learned very much. He can just about manage to order two coffees. '*Due espresso*,' he ventures.

'Almost,' says Emilio. 'But it is "*espresso*" only for one coffee. Two coffees is "*espressi*."'

'Ah, yes. I see. Perhaps you would like to give me lessons?'

'I'd be happy to do so. When would you like to begin?'

Charles suggests that there's no time like the present, but first he would like to have a nightcap, and perhaps Emilio would like to join him. So they agree to conduct the lessons there in the lobby over two whiskies.

'It is the drink of your country, yes?'

'One of the best things to come out of Scotland,' Charles confirms.

'*Dove andrete domani?*'

'Sorry?'

'Where are you going tomorrow?'

'Oh, *Io e Margaret*... are going?'

'*andremo*'

'... *andremo in treno a Pisa*.'

'*Molto buono*.'

* * *

The train journey to Pisa takes two hours. Charles is most anxious to see what Margaret will make of it, since she insisted they go, in spite of his having been very dismissive of both the cathedral and the Leaning Tower.

'I know what you think of it,' she argues. 'But I want to form my own opinion.'

Her husband silently mouths a comment, and she smiles to herself as she knows he has just said, 'You won't like it.'

They ascend the famous tower and enjoy the disconcerting feeling of being off the horizontal. Afterwards, they walk together over the lawns of the cathedral precinct, Charles hardly daring to open his mouth. They peep inside the cathedral, but Margaret's reluctance to spend much time there speaks volumes.

'Have a look at the choir stalls, though,' says Charles.

Margaret examines the intricate carvings on the end of the walnut benches.

'These are quite exquisite,' she agrees. 'What a lovely rich colour the wood is.'

'These are the best examples of woodwork that I've seen here,' says Charles. 'Usually, they don't pay sufficient attention to the grain of the wood and its delicacy. It's as if the carving has been done by masons, using the same techniques as they would on a block of stone or marble.'

'You're right. It's often too... robust.'

Returning outside they appraise the arcaded façades of the cathedral, the leaning tower and the cemetery wall beyond. Charles is anxious to know Margaret's verdict.

'Well, it is a little repetitive...'

'Just a little.'

She wonders if she can maintain the pretence of not already knowing his opinion, because he has already told her – more often, probably, than he remembers – that he found the repeated motif of arcaded columns overplayed in the extreme. She recalls him saying that there was nowhere to rest the eye.

'There is no sense of composition, is there?' she says at length. 'When I think of the way that you balanced one form against another. Here it is merely one solution played out *ad infinitum*.'

'*Ad nauseam*.'

'Well, we are agreed.'

'I like the Baptistry, though.'

Margaret is surprised. The round tiered building is competent, and nicely executed, although she thought Charles would, like her, find it too rich a confection, like a wedding cake resplendent in embellishments of white royal icing.

But as her gaze lingers on the building, it begins to revolve slowly and a strange sensation of dizziness overtakes her. For a moment, the leaning tower appears to have returned to the upright position and she has to grab Charles's arm to steady herself.

'Are you all right, Margaret?'

'No, I...' And the next moment she is on the grass. Several passers-by stop to look and two come running over. Charles can't think how he can best help her, and is relieved when Margaret opens her eyes and says, 'I'm all right... all right.'

He manages to get her back on her feet and, with her leaning on him for support, assists her as far as a little bench, where she decides to spend a few more minutes. From nowhere, a young woman appears carrying a glass of water.

'Thank you. *Grazie*.'

'Would you like some more?' she asks, offering to return to wherever she came from for a refill.

'No, I'm all right. Really. *Molto grazie*.'

Charles asks her what she thinks is the matter.

'Probably too much sun,' she says, and certainly they have been guilty of failing to take any account of the strong sun, shining consistently in a clear sky for the last two days. Unlike most of their compatriots, they haven't been taking every opportunity to seek out the shade.

'Wait here,' says Charles. 'Don't move.' And he runs off across the grass with his awkward limping gait.

Ten minutes later, he returns carrying a large black umbrella.

Margaret smiles at him. 'Goodness, Toshie. Are you expecting rain?'

'When in Rome,' says Charles and as Margaret is about to protest, continues, 'well I know this isn't actually Rome, but you must have noticed. Practically all the Italians carry umbrellas, rain or shine. I've never seen such a thing.

Not just the middle classes – the taxi drivers, the tradesmen, the shopkeepers. Everyone.' He fumbles with the catch until, at last, the canopy of the umbrella springs open. 'I asked them if they had a Royal Drooko, but they didn't seem to know what I was talking about.'

Despite her residual dizziness, Margaret wants to laugh at the thought of Charles trying to explain to a puzzled shop-keeper in his pidgin Italian what a Drooko was. She accepts his help to get to her feet and, taking the umbrella from him, holds it above her head. 'Don't I look a bit silly, doing this in the blazing sunshine?'

'Not at all. You're not the only one – look!' And, sure enough, there are other groups of tourists sheltering under black umbrellas.

'Plus,' he continues, 'if you feel a bit unsteady on your feet, you can use it as a walking stick, and nobody will imagine that you are anything but fighting fit.'

'Well, thank you, Toshie.' She twirls the umbrella like a parasol and they set off carefully, in the direction of the railway station.

Unfortunately, the incident proves not to be an isolated one. Margaret suffers a similar attack the next day, and the day after, and, since the skies have become overcast, they can no longer blame these occurrences on the sun.

'You must see a doctor,' says Charles, and Margaret promises to do just that as soon as they get back to Port-Vendres.

CHAPTER 12

MARGARET STIRS IN the bedroom of her lodging in Bramerton Street, in the slightly uncomfortable bed that has accommodated her for the last week. The grey, grainy darkness is beginning to give way to definable forms within the room. There is a narrow, vertical slit of daylight between the curtains.

'Four more weeks,' she thinks. 'Then I'm back in the sunshine.'

The doctor in Port-Vendres had given her bad news. He told her she had a heart condition which, from he the way he described it in his broken English, she understood to be arrhythmia – an irregularity of the heartbeat which, on occasion, could result in a malfunction such as that she had experienced in Italy. There were various treatments available, but the one that he recommended involved a series of mild electric shocks to stimulate the muscle and regain its regularity. He knew of a clinic in London where this could be effected and said he would be pleased to give her a letter confirming his diagnosis.

She had wasted no time in contacting Patrick Geddes, who told her, yes, the clinic that the French doctor had recommended was one that he himself had attended and for which he had a high regard. Charles argued that they should both make the trip, but Margaret could see no sense in this. There were a number of things that she could attend to while she was in London: she needed to visit a dentist, and she could even go up to Liverpool to see Frances and Bertie's solicitor about some outstanding details regarding Frances's estate. If Charles accompanied her, he would only be kicking his heels, anxious to get back to his painting.

Besides which, they could ill afford the subsistence, whereas his living expenses in France would be minimal.

'I think the breadwinner should go on earning the bread,' she told him. 'We can't both go gallivanting about like a pair of tourists.'

But she misses him, more than she thought she would.

She turns on to her back and stares at the ceiling. The duties she had taken on board have proven quite exhausting. Charles gave her three of his pictures to see if she could get them exhibited, and hopefully sold, because they could really use the extra income, and when her course of dental treatment was finished, she had decided to get that task out of the way next.

First, she had to return to Chapman Brothers in King's Road where she had left the pictures the previous week to get them framed. Charles's instructions for mounts had been quite explicit, and she worried in case Mr Chapman might try and impose his own ideas. But no, he agreed that a thick mount would greatly enhance the sense of depth, and she felt she could trust him to honour Charles's wishes. The next hurdle was to ensure that any gallery owner who agreed to hang them would do so in the way that they deserved, since, on one occasion, some of Charles's flower paintings had been disgracefully exhibited at the Grafton Gallery. As she was leaving the framers, the gathering clouds began to look threatening, so she took the bus to Leicester Square, and by the time she alighted it was raining steadily. Although she had had the foresight to bring an umbrella, the parcelled-up paintings made it difficult to deal with, so she decided not to open it up until she had dropped them off, and quickened her pace, hoping that the gallery would accept them. When she finally arrived, she waited just inside the door while the receptionist fetched one of the directors.

'Ah, Mrs Mackintosh. We spoke on the phone. How nice to meet you. Would you like to bring the pictures upstairs?'

She followed the dapper gentleman up the staircase and into an empty room where a large table had been placed against the wall opposite the window. He stood by the window with his elbow on his wrist and his chin on his hand, and waited while Margaret unwrapped each of the three parcels, placing them finally on the table, propped up against the wall. For a while he appraised them, saying nothing, walking up close to the paintings and then standing back. She became aware of her heart racing and wondered if this might be dangerous.

Finally, he spoke.

'These are very nice, Mrs Mackintosh. Very nice indeed. You said your husband painted them?'

'He's an architect.' As an afterthought she added, 'Retired, of course. That one was painted in Port-Vendres in France, where we live, and the other in Fetges, in the Cerdagne valley.'

'I like the frames, and the mounts as well. Did he choose the mounts?'

Margaret said that he had, and that the thick card was to his specification.

'And I see they're signed.'

'Yes.' Margaret thought it best not to reveal that, with Charles's agreement, it was she that had signed them.

'I should think we can exhibit these. They show a modernity, which is a desirable feature these days. There should be some interest. This one might fetch twenty pounds, and I'd place the other – where did you say that was done?'

'Fetges.'

'I would put it at around thirty pounds. Of course, I can't guarantee that they would sell.'

Margaret felt relieved. 'No, of course. When do you think you can show them?'

'That I don't know at the moment. Could you leave them with us? Sybil will give you a receipt before you leave. You know our commission is thirty per cent?'

She didn't know, but she nodded. 'That's all right. Yes, I will leave them, thank you.'

It was a weight lifted, off her arms as well as her mind.

*　　*　　*

Margaret reaches over to switch on the bedside lamp and lifts the thick sheaf of letters from the cabinet, held together with an elastic band. Every day Charles has recorded the minutiae of his solitary existence in the Roussillon, calling this his 'Chronycle', and peppering it with his accustomed idiosyncratic spelling and punctuation. She hasn't fully absorbed the latest one and slides it out so she can peruse it again.

> Another big ship has come in today – the *Acola* from Valencia, and the *Poupée* has just returned. So on our side we have the *Poupée*, the *Acola*, the *Esperos* and the *Danielito*. On the other side a Greek ship – the *Thermes* – and two Italians from Messina – names unknown. So you see our harbour is very full – and you can hear and see the activity of women, children and men all day long.

> Monsieur Déjean has been giving me lots of the little grey cherries – I like these very much. He always suggests wild & semi-wild little things to eat – a great plate of asparagus – all purple tops and no green. Actually, they're too perfect: not a flaw, not a defect, but unfortunately not much flavour. But he served some lovely young goat that was very good indeed.

> This morning I was singing a dirge and Rosa told me I should be crying instead of singing – but she did not realise that I was singing sadly. I'm afraid that Kim is looking for a job at Font Romeu – apart from what we give him, he has not made 10 francs this month. So he's trying to learn one English word at every meal – today's

word was 'vinegar' – at that rate he will speak a little English two hundred years from now.

Last night I was standing on the balcony having an animated conversation in French with Madame and Monsieur Déjean, much to their amusement and much to my exhaustion – still, it is good for the French which I must speak sometimes.

If one is seeking tranquillity for work, the weather here just now is ideal: clear blue sky, brilliant sun, and clean pure air blown at you and through you. Absolutely perfect!

*　*　*

She is practically the last in the breakfast room, the other tables having already been cleared. As Margaret dips her strip of toast into her soft-boiled egg, Miss Delmege comes up to her, and places an envelope beside her plate.

'Another letter from France, Mrs Mackintosh. Your husband is a most proliferous writer!' There is a slight edge to her smile. Margaret wonders if she imagines that the letters are not from her husband at all? For a fleeting moment, she is tempted play on this: 'No, Miss Delmege, between ourselves, these are not from my husband. I have a lover...' She decides, however, that it might be a little unfair on Toshie.

As she empties the last of the tea into her cup, she tries to prepare mentally for her interview with Mr Barman of the *Architects' Journal*. Charles had asked her in one of his letters if she wouldn't mind doing this for him. She had mixed feelings about it, but agreed to see Mr Barman, and so telephoned to arrange a meeting. He had suggested the lounge of Claridge's at two o'clock this afternoon.

*　*　*

It's almost dark by the time Margaret gets to Callow Street, where Meg and Fergusson have a house in the elegant terrace. She feels exhausted. Fergusson opens the door and welcomes her in his usual effusive manner.

'Margaret! Come in, come in. How lovely to see you. Meg's in the kitchen, preparing something sumptuous for us. Come in!'

She lets him take her coat and precedes him through to the lounge, where, falling into an easy chair, she allows the warm relaxing feeling that comes from being once more among friends to overtake her.

'So, Margaret. How has your day been?'

'My day,' says Margaret, 'has been spent acting as my husband's press officer.' She gives him a look that suggests it hadn't been a role she greatly relished. Fergusson sits down opposite her and waits for the rest of the story.

'The *AJ*,' she says, ' – sorry, the *Architects' Journal* – contacted Toshie in France and asked him for his comments on the state of modern English Architecture, and he replied by saying simply that there isn't any. Of course, when they said "English", I'm sure they meant "British".'

'I think he's right,' says Fergusson. 'When a certain architect left Glasgow, I think the contemporary design of buildings came to an end. Everything now is just a pastiche of former styles.'

'Well, that's just about the size of it,' Margaret agrees. 'Toshie said, rightly in my opinion, that if Mr Barman wanted to see modern architecture, he would have to go to Europe. Look what Mies and Gropius are up to at the Bauhaus, and Corbusier in France. That's where it's all happening.'

'So what did you have to say to Mr Barman?'

'Well, Toshie rather dumped me in it, didn't he? I tried to answer his questions as best I could, but it wasn't easy. I told him I felt as if he was talking to the wrong person.'

The door opens and Meg emerges from the kitchen, wearing an apron. She kisses Margaret and is slightly taken aback when the kiss is returned on both of her cheeks.

'Sorry, Meg,' says Margaret. 'I've got into the French habit.'

'I remember, Loïs used to do that, too. Excuse me spending time in the kitchen. I hope Fergus is entertaining you.'

'I was just telling him about my interview with the *Architects' Journal*. The damned man wanted to know what made Toshie give up his practice in Glasgow, and I think he found me a little evasive.'

'Quite right!' says Meg. 'None of his damn business.'

'He asked me if Toshie bore a grudge against Keppie, and I said I didn't think that he did. But I said he should go and speak to Keppie, because I certainly had no intention of talking ill of the man, even if he does deserve it. Excuse me a minute, I've written it all down.'

She pulls her handbag towards her and takes out a little notebook.

'To make matters worse, he wanted to know all about Charles Reilly. What could the Professor of Architecture at Liverpool have done to upset Toshie?'

Fergusson's curiosity is piqued. 'Well? What did he do?'

'It was a number of things really. He didn't exactly do my brother-in-law Bertie any favours while he was there, and he's made various inappropriate comments about architecture in the press.'

'Didn't Toshie feel Reilly had excluded him unfairly from the Liverpool Cathedral competition?' asks Meg.

'That's right. He never forgave him for that.'

'So Toshie must have given Barman a hint of this at some point?' suggests Fergusson.

'Not exactly. He thought he was being subtle. He didn't refer to him by name, but he called him something like "that well-known loudspeaker from Liverpool" and said that he understands as much about what he was the professor of, as the mechanical instrument of the same name understands of what he is shouting through it.'

Fergusson laughs. 'Oh, heavens. That doesn't leave much doubt, does it? He hasn't printed it, has he?'

'I'm sure he won't. The *AJ* doesn't really go in for controversy, and what would be the point of exposing yourself to claims of libel?'

Meg decides it's time to change the subject. 'I've got something for you, Margaret.' She reaches into a drawer, takes out a book, and passes it across to her friend.

'For me? How intriguing!'

It's entitled *Margaret Morris Dancing* and inside the cover there's an inscription, 'To Margaret and Toshie with much love and best of wishes always – from Meg – June 1927'.

Margaret thumbs through the pages. 'How wonderful, Meg. When did you publish this?'

'About eighteen months ago. We'd been working on it for some time, and I almost forgot I kept a copy for you.'

'But, what a wonderful present. Toshie will be delighted! I am, too. Thank you.'

She puts the book into her handbag and snaps the clasp shut.

'So, tell me,' Meg asks. 'How did you get on with your dentist?'

'That feels like a long time ago already. Yes, he was excellent. Thank you so much for recommending him. For some reason, Toshie insists on calling him the Butcher with the White Face – it must have been something I said – but anyway he also said not to worry about the cost, so long as he has everything fixed by June.'

'And everything's fixed?'

'Pretty well. I have a couple of gaps...' she shows Meg where the extractions were made, 'but no pain anymore, which is the main thing.'

'So, how is Toshie?' asks Fergusson. 'Apart from making you his press secretary, does he tell you much about what he's up to in France?'

Margaret smiles. 'He has made it his religion. I get a letter from him practically every day.'

'Good gracious!'

'I confess I feel rather guilty if I don't send him a daily reply.'

*　　*　　*

Meg excuses herself, and returns shortly to suggest that they take their places at the table. As Fergusson dispenses the wine, Meg begins to ferry dishes of vegetables and potatoes. Rising, Margaret asks if she can assist, but Meg pushes down on her shoulders.

'No, stay there. Only the pie to come.'

The pie is brought forth from the kitchen with great ceremony and Meg places it gently on a mat at the end of the table. 'I hope you like steak and kidney.'

Margaret says it's one of her favourites, but Fergusson tells her he can't be doing with kidneys at all, so he's made his own arrangements. And with that he slides a smaller dish on to his place mat.

'Purchased today from that butcher on the King's Road,' says Meg. 'You must have seen his kidneys in the window. I've often looked longingly at them on the way past.'

'Well!' says her husband, 'It's just as well he wasn't displaying any other part of his anatomy!'

Meg gives him a look with a sideways glance at Margaret thinking she might not approve of Fergus's rather ribald sense of humour. But she needn't have worried. Margaret has a broad smile on her face.

'Anyway,' she continues, 'today I gave in.'

'It looks wonderful,' says Margaret.

'Well,' Meg digs her serving spoon through the crust of pastry, 'let's hope it's as good as it looks.'

But later, after Fergusson has accompanied her back to Miss Delmege's, Margaret begins to feel a queasy sensation in her stomach which presages a night of visits to the toilet at the end of the corridor.

CHAPTER 13

ALTHOUGH IT'S ANOTHER fine sunny morning in Port-Vendres, when Charles steps outside with his bag of equipment he realises that the wind is too strong to make painting a practical proposition. Instead, he decides to walk over to Collioure with some books about Matisse that he has borrowed from Edgar Hereford.

It's a pleasant two-mile walk along the coast, but when he arrives at the boys' lodgings he finds them deserted. Another guest who is staying in Madame's apartments sees his perplexed expression.

'Are you looking for Ihlee?' she asks in English.

'Yes. Ihlee or Hereford. Do you know if they're around?'

'Afraid not. They've gone off to Perpignan with Madame.'

'Ah… I wonder if you would be so kind as to hand these in to Hereford when you see him?'

The woman says that would be no problem.

'*Merci bien, madame.*'

And so, wondering why he has just spoken in French to an English woman, he begins his homeward journey to Port-Vendres. He is just entering the port when he sees Rudolph striding down the road from the station towards him.

'Ah, Toshie. *Bonne après midi!*'

It's a habit we all get into, thinks Charles. Perhaps not a bad one.

'Edgar and I are just back from Perpignan,' says Ihlee. 'Took Madame for a day out. It pays to stay in her good books, you know.'

'I'm sure,' says Charles. 'I'm just back from Collioure myself. I left Edgar's books with a neighbour.'

'Ah, sorry about that. Listen, we thought we'd come over to your place tonight for a spot of dinner. All right with you?'

Charles says that would be fine, although part of him feels he doesn't really have a choice, and if he had, he might have opted for a night on his own. Still, he supposes it will stop him from sitting alone at the table, feeling sorry for himself.

The two boys duly turn up for dinner, both dressed in the current fashion with blue jackets and matching blue shirts and ties. Monsieur Déjean does them proud as usual, providing an excellent soup, before serving them chicken with asparagus and onions. Then stewed prunes for dessert followed by biscuits and Roquefort cheese.

'How is Margaret getting on in London?' asks Rudolph.

'She's doing well, bless her. She's left some of my pictures at the Leicester Galleries. We're rather hoping they're going to be able to exhibit them soon. Fergie told her he was extremely sorry he couldn't have been more help to her in that sense, but what could he have done?'

'Fergus has got himself established, hasn't he?' says Edgar. 'I don't suppose he remembers what it was like before.'

'I'm sure he remembers very well,' says Charles, 'but he's pretty tied up at the moment with all these visits to America. And at the end of the day, you just have to do the legwork. At least, poor Margaret does, anyway.'

'So does Margaret write to you?' Rudolph now asks.

'Almost every day. She's spent some time with Fergus and Meg, and she's been in touch with the Schwabes, of course.'

'Oh, how are Randolph and Birdie?' Edgar wants to know. He recalls them from the many afternoon gatherings of artists in the Blue Cockatoo, where everyone called Gwendolen by the nickname that somehow suits her perfectly.

'They're fine, by all accounts. We were rather hoping they'd be able to join us in Mont Louis later in the year.'

'And do you write to Margaret?' asks Rudolph, clearly expecting a shamefaced denial from Charles.

'I write every day. But I don't send a letter every day, because the postage is expensive,' he admits, 'although I'm working at keeping my handwriting very small, to save paper, and thereby to save money, both on the paper and the postage.'

Edgar guffaws, thinking that Charles is joking, and then has the grace to look embarrassed when he realises that money really is an issue for him.

'But you miss her?' he asks.

Charles places his hand on Edgar's arm. 'It's hard to describe how much. It's as if part of me is missing. I am incomplete.'

'So, when is she coming back?' asks Rudolph.

'On the 30th. We're going to rendezvous at Perpignan Station, and then take the train back up to Mont Louis. By then it will be too hot here for us both.'

'Then we'll miss you,' says Edgar.

'I'm sure you mean that sincerely, but I think for you the word has a different sense from how I'm using it of Margaret.'

The two men try and think of something to lighten the mood.

'Isn't your birthday coming up soon?' asks Rudolph. 'We'll have to have a gala to celebrate.'

Charles makes a dismissive gesture, but Edgar presses him for the date, which is still a fortnight away on the 7th of June.

'Well, then. Let's have a party. Come on over to ours, and we'll have something organised. Perhaps Madame will kill the fatted calf. What would you like as a present?'

'A present? Fifty-nine is far too old for presents. At my age I have everything I need.'

Rudolph frowns at him. 'Didn't I hear Margaret say you could do with a stool? For when you're painting in the open air?'

'Margaret is very good at telling me what I need, but...'

'But I have a stool,' says Rudolph. 'It folds up very small, so it's just the job for carrying around with all your other gear. I never use it now, because I never paint outdoors.'

'Oh, I couldn't possibly...' says Charles.

'Well, that's settled, then. You can have my stool for your birthday.'

*   *   *

A few days later, Charles is lingering over his breakfast while Kim begins to clear the tables. He lifts a couple of saucers, looks at Charles and says what sounds like 'soassers?' Charles corrects him, makes him repeat the word and then tells him that the other dishes are not 'plats' but 'plates'. A young man who has been nursing a brandy at the bar, sidles over and stands next to Charles's table as if waiting for something.

'Can I help you?' says Charles, without getting up.

The young man puts a hand on the table, leans in towards Charles, and says something in French which Charles can't grasp at all. So he calls Kim back over to translate.

'He wishes to know if you would permit him to join you at dinner, and tell him the names of everything in English, the same as you do for me.'

Charles is uneasy. 'No, *non,*' he says, getting to his feet. 'For you, Kim, it is a pleasure, but I am not going to teach English to the whole of Port-Vendres. I need to have peace and quiet when I'm eating. Tranquillity, Kim.' He doesn't realise that his voice is getting louder, as if this will make up for his lack of French. 'Please, Kim. Tell him *non*!'

At this point Monsieur Déjean comes over to see what the problem is, and Kim, who was slightly disconcerted by

Charles's reaction, explains the situation to his boss. To Charles's surprise, this results in the owner rounding on the young man and ordering him to return to the bar, which he duly does, his tail between his legs.

'I'm sorry, Monsieur,' says Charles, concerned that he has over-reacted. 'I didn't mean to be unfriendly. I just need to have my...' he searches for the word in French, but it won't come. '... my tranquillity.'

'No, no, Monsieur Mackintosh. It is I who apologise to you, that you have been disturbed in this fashion!'

'That's fine, Monsieur. *Merci*.' And Charles, happy to leave it at that, is just about to mount the stairs up to his room, when Madame Déjean emerges from the kitchen. As soon as her husband apprises her of what has taken place, she too is indignant.

'Monsieur Mackintosh,' she says, '*je suis désolé que vous ayez été dérangé*.' Now she turns to her mother who is standing just behind her, and tells her all about the situation. Charles understands not one word of the conversation, but can tell that Granny is equally affronted. The whole family follows Charles up to the landing, where Rosa has just finished making his bed.

As soon as he sees her, Monsieur Déjean narrates the whole tale again for her benefit.

'Oh, Monsieur. I am so sorry for you,' says Rosa, and for a while the five of them stand outside Charles's room, reviewing the recent event with much gesticulation, giving it far more significance than Charles ever imagined it warranted.

Eventually, Monsieur Déjean pats Charles's arm and tells him he can be sure that it won't happen again. 'I personally will do everything to make certain that you will not be disturbed, Monsieur Mackintosh. You will have your... tranquillity.'

'Tranquillity... Yes. Thank you, Monsieur Déjean.'

Charles enters his room and closes the door, more than a little bemused. All he needs is some peace and quiet, and up until a half-hour ago, he had them both in spades. He isn't sure that the French have quite grasped the concept of tranquillity, but at least it seems that he's unlikely to be disturbed again.

* * *

Now, feeling completely calm and savouring his hard-earned peace, Charles strolls out on to the quay with his painting equipment and sets off along the south side of the harbour to the location of what he calls his 'Rock'. He has high hopes of making progress with his picture.

But hardly has he established himself when a bunch of schoolboys appear, all curious to know what he is doing. Though their curiosity is easily satisfied, nevertheless they persist in hanging around like a group of settlers who have come upon a native and wish to draw from his experience. He wonders if he has, after all, what they call a magnetic personality.

Charles keeps hoping that they will get bored and go off to paddle or fish, but the minutes tick by and they show no sign of moving, chattering to each other instead like a group of monkeys. He finds it impossible to concentrate, and considers getting up and shouting incomprehensibly at them, waving his paintbrush like a sword, but is put off this course of action by the thought that they might find him funny and only be encouraged to stay. Eventually they start to get up, brushing the grass of their school clothes, and slowly amble away, perhaps to return to their lessons.

But, for Charles, the moment of inspiration has fled and instead a cloud of depression settles on him, making him wonder if this might be the pattern from now on, his famous and hard-earned tranquillity threatened at every turn.

The next minute he hears his name being called and turns to see Rudolph Ihlee emerging from the tunnel.

'Toshie! This is where you are! How are you getting on?'

'Hello, Rudolph.'

Rudolph walks up to the easel and is immediately impressed by what he sees. 'By Jove, that's rather fine. I like the texture of the rock. It looks almost... alive.'

'Well, that's what I was aiming for. I want to make it appear like a kind of organic building – a construction growing out of the landscape.'

'So, it appeals to the architect in you?'

'You saw my Moorish Fort? That was a building that looked like part of the landscape. This, by contrast, is to be part of the landscape that looks like a building.'

Rudolph takes a step back to give the picture his full critical appraisal. 'Possibly a little too much green there, Toshie,' he says; but he has a twinkle in his eye, and Charles knows that his previous self-criticism has been noted and is now returning as a jest.

After a while, Rudolph sits down beside him. 'You know, Toshie. You really are a marvel. You never seem depressed. You're always cheerful and happy. I was feeling quite gloomy earlier, but you've cheered me up no end.'

'What do you have to be depressed about?' Charles asks him.

'Oh, I just get a bit downhearted sometimes. I think I really need a change, so I thought about moving up to Quillan. Do you know it? It's on the River Aude about 40 kilometres north of Mont Louis. There's the famous Pierre Lys Gorge, and I thought it might be jolly to have a go at painting it for a month or two. But Edgar doesn't want to go, and I don't seem to be able to persuade him.'

'Why don't you go without him?' asks Charles.

Rudolph is surprised that Charles even has to ask. 'It would be dismal on my own, Toshie. I'm afraid I'm not content with my own company like you are.'

Charles just gives him a look, thinking perhaps he himself is better than he thought at concealing his intense loneliness.

* * *

In the evening, when Charles writes to his wife, he tells her about the forthcoming party, but says he wishes he were spending it with her. Perhaps he has a foreboding that the gala won't be to his liking. He sets off at seven o'clock and enjoys the coastal walk in the balmy early evening air. As he approaches Madame's apartments, he sees Rudolph across the road carrying two bottles of champagne.

'Good timing, Toshie! Come and have a look at my new studio. Hang on, I'll just get rid of these.' He takes them inside and reappears moments later, slightly out of breath. 'Those stairs will be the death of me. Now, it's just around the corner.'

It is only a short walk to the building where the boys have rented two rooms on the first floor to use as studios. 'Somewhere we can be as messy as we like without having to clear up at the end of each day,' explains Rudolph.

Ihlee's studio has a large window on one wall, and the open roof structure is perforated with skylights. A large easel in one corner is covered with a sheet, and Charles notices that there is a large number of canvasses stacked against the walls.

'I like it,' says Charles. 'It's a great space.'

'I'm going to see if I can take away those cupboards along the back wall. That would give the room a better proportion, don't you think?'

Charles nods his agreement.

'But on the whole, I'm delighted.' He lowers his voice. 'Edgar's making do with the other one on the other side of the passage. Come and have a look.'

Hereford is there, finishing his day's work.

'Come in, Toshie. I'm just going to wash these brushes, then I'll be right with you. What do you make of my workspace?'

It is immediately apparent that Hereford's studio is the better of the two. Even in the gathering dusk, Charles can tell that it will benefit from good daylight.

'It's very fine,' he says. 'I'm beginning to envy you chaps. Now you have no excuse at all for not turning out the most excellent pictures.'

There is a pregnant pause as Charles is about to turn back towards the stairs, assuming that a party awaits him at the boys' apartments. But he just catches sight of Edgar giving Rudolph a meaningful look, and realises that something must be amiss.

'What is it?'

'Well, we bought a leg of lamb yesterday, and asked Madame if she would cook it for us,' explains Rudolph. 'Only...'

'We've had a sort of falling out,' says Edgar.

'Oh?'

'You know what a lovely evening it was last night? We had a few girls over for some drinks and it got a bit noisy, so Madame came up to see what was going on. And she seemed to take exception to one of the girls.'

'You mean...?'

'A lady of somewhat loose virtue,' says Rudolph.

'I see.'

'So, she told us to get rid of her, or she would call the police.'

'And, did you?'

'Well, we sort of said we would, but in the event, she left anyway.'

'After a couple of hours,' adds Edgar.

'And was Madame all right with that?'

'Ah... well. That's the thing,' says Rudolph. 'We're not entirely sure if we're fully back on speaking terms.'

There is another general shifting of feet and scratching of heads, until Rudolph says, 'So, we wondered if you...?'

'You want me to go and talk to her and see if the dinner is on or off?'

'Would you?'

Charles felt as if he didn't have much choice. They headed back to the apartments together and the boys went upstairs while Charles knocked on Madame's door. It was opened so suddenly that he wondered if she had been watching at the window.

'Ah, Monsieur Mackintosh. I am enchanted to see you. You are the birthday boy today, *n'est-ce pas?*'

'*Oui, vous avez raison.*'

'It is good that these boys have a friend like you, Monsieur. They need a – how do you say? – a steadying influence.'

'I'm not sure that I...'

'Because, you see, they are both very fond of the...' she pantomimes the raising of a glass.

'Well, they're young, and...'

'They have been drinking – how you say? – like the fish for the last three weeks.'

Charles can't think of any appropriate response.

'And they are also very fond of the...' and this time her hands outline the curvaceous body of a young lady.

'Well, they're young, Madame. *Et ils ont besoin de jeunes femmes.*'

'*Oui, bien sûr. Mais* there are *jeunes femmes*, and there are *jeunes femmes.*'

'Well, anyway. They are both very sorry that they upset you last night.'

Madame makes a dismissive gesture, and proceeds to give forth in an outflow of French, which Charles cannot follow at all, but assumes that it was a diatribe against young women of doubtful morals.

When she seems to have finished, he coughs and says, 'So now they are wondering...'

She begins again. Another tirade, no more comprehensible than the first. Finally, she looks at Charles as if she expects him to say something.

He decides to hedge his bets. 'I totally agree with you, Madame. I have suggested to Ihlee and Hereford that, while they are guests in your house, they should respect your rules.'

This seems to appease her.

'So...?' Charles clears his throat again, hoping that she can guess why he's come and save him the embarrassment of asking. But she's not giving an inch.

'The arrangement they made with you yesterday? Dinner? Here, tonight?' He wishes his French was up to making his question sound more diplomatic.

'*Oui, bien sûr.*'

It is a positive response, but it sounds grudging.

'*Merci beaucoup, Madame.* I shall go and tell them.'

* * *

The leg of lamb has been cooked to perfection and falls off the bone. The sauce is full of interesting flavours, and Madame has also provided a selection of fresh tender vegetables, which she serves as a separate course. But, despite the champagne, the atmosphere in which the meal is eaten is strained.

'This is wonderful, Madame,' says Charles, trying to lighten the mood.

The boys nod in agreement, their mouths full, but Madame makes no effort to reply. As she concentrates on her plate, Charles makes a desperate signal to Rudolph that he should attempt some sort of conversation.

'Delicious,' says Rudolph, and Charles casts his eyes to heaven in despair.

'Yes, absolutely delicious,' says Edgar, and he continues to eat.

No sooner have they finished their meal than Rudolph announces that they have just taken delivery of a set of recordings of Paderewski playing Beethoven. 'You must come and hear them, Toshie,' he says. 'We've set the gramophone up in my studio.'

Unceremoniously, they get up from the table and take their leave of Madame's apartment, rather overly eager to be excused from the icy atmosphere.

Listening to the *Emperor Concerto*, they set about finishing the second bottle of champagne.

Half way through the record, Rudolph leaves the room to answer a call of nature, and Charles takes the opportunity to satisfy his curiosity about Edgar's car repair.

'Did you manage to get your car fixed, Hereford? It needed a new bonnet, didn't it?'

'Oh, yes. That was last year. The hood was quite badly twisted.'

'And how did that happen?'

Edgar looked over his shoulder to make sure that Rudolph was still out of the room, and replied in a confidential tone. 'Actually, Toshie, my car got damaged in the same accident as Ihlee's, but it wasn't me who was driving it. Mine is more powerful and faster than his, and he'd been itching to have a go at it for weeks; so he'd asked me if we could swap for the journey home from Perpignan. Which wasn't really a good idea since we'd both had a drink or two.'

'Ah, I see. So it was you who ran into the back of the strawberry cart?'

'As Ihlee said, it was the last thing we expected to see on that road at that time of night. And he was following far too close behind. So...!'

Charles indicates a collision by driving his right fist into his left palm.

'Precisely', says Edgar. 'Rudolph's car ran straight into the strawberry cart, and mine into the back of his.' He lowers his voice. 'Don't tell him I told you. He's rather embarrassed.'

As the concerto thunders to a climax, Rudolph rejoins them and there are inebriated smiles all round. They agree it is an excellent performance.

Finally, Charles feels able to plead that his extreme age, at least compared with theirs, makes him weary at this hour, and he manages to escape in time to get back to the Hôtel du Commerce just before midnight.

CHAPTER 14

DEAR MARGARET,

This morning was very grey, with great mists driving in from the sea. Rosa said it would not clear, but I went out anyway and, after my waiting patiently, the fog cleared at about half-past ten, so I was able to finish our 'Fort'. That is a great relief. I wish I could also finish my 'Rock.' Then it could be put away. I really like putting away finished pictures, better than saving money. When I was walking up towards the fort, I saw the new people going to the cottage in the pine wood. They were leading a young kid and a little lamb on a string, and when I came back they were both hanging on a tree, skinned and ready for the evening meal. That's one thing a camper should learn: instead of walking to buy your *viandes*, you should make your *viandes* walk to you.

A squadron arrived yesterday quite unexpectedly and anchored just off that promontory called The Mole: two big battle ships, the *Lorraine* and the *Strasbourg*, and four destroyers, *Hora, Somali, Annamite* and *Touareg*. You know how news travels here without a newspaper, so they were expecting crowds last night and today. Next thing you know, there were motorboats, sailing boats, steamboats, motor cars, motor wagons and horse-drawn, mule-drawn and donkey-drawn carts, all arriving with crowds of people to see our 'Glorious Youth' of the squadron. Poor Kim couldn't go home because there were so many people.

It has rained all day and the visit of the squadron has been a terrible failure as far as Kim is concerned and, I suppose, on a much larger scale, for the Hotel. Kim says that he wasn't allowed to go home for his day off and that if it had been a good sunny day he would have – then he rubs his great big thumb on his first two fingers and says 'Pah' or something like that. Nevertheless, the young sailor lads – hundreds and hundreds of them – have made a feeble hearted French effort to paint the town red – white and blue. The four torpedo boats that were in the harbour left tonight just at seven o'clock, and I think (as far as I saw) there were only three young sailors – routed out of brothels and pubs – who had to be carried on board struggling and protesting – by the naval police patrol. There were hundreds of others that just managed to get on board in a jolly state that reminded me of scenes I have seen in Plymouth or Falmouth when my visits to these ancient seaports coincided with a visit by some battleships of the British navy.

Another little Spanish sailing ship has come in (of the sewing machine species) named the Comercio. It is crammed full of wine – as Monsieur Marty says, they have never had so much wine coming into the port. Most of it goes to Perpignan. Monsieur Marty tells me that the stevedores make 50 francs per day when they are working, which is unfortunately not every day; it is equivalent to what a bricklayer can get in England, but he can normally work every day in the week. The women who work on the ships unloading beans etc only get half of that because they are usually the wives of the men. What happened to equal pay for equal work?

I was very glad to get your letter and very sorry to hear of the steak and kidney pie incident. My God, these multi-coloured kidneys we used to see in the Butcher's shop on King's Road made one sick just to look at them. How wise of Fergie to make his own pot – that steak and kidney pie makes me feel sick even here. It distresses me to learn that you do not feel so well. You be very careful and rest as much as you can.

Your letter is interesting because you say that Fergie liked my pictures – I don't think that there is any artist I would like to please better than Fergusson, and Margaret Morris also – but these are not the opinions that make money and I want to make a little just to give to you. How nice it would be, Margaret, if I could give you just a little, or a lot would be better. I hope that in some way Fergusson's approval and the prospect of a show at the Leicester Galleries will compensate you in a small way for all the trouble you have had with my damned pictures.

I am glad to know that Fergusson had a success in America and is going to have another show – I am still sure that he is one of the very good painters and I hope he will have a financial success this time in London. It is a pity Meg is tied to London, otherwise Fergie could be anywhere and paint quite as well if not better (and at the same time have a better life) than he can in Callow Street. I shall be glad to see Fergusson's catalogue and shall be most careful to send it back when I have finished.

Rosa is asking me mysteriously to let her know in lots of time when you are coming back so that she can prepare your room.

MMYT

Dear Toshie

Thank you for your letters. You are most assiduous, and I'm afraid I cannot match your dedication, or keep up with replying to all your questions.

I am having to move my lodgings, as Miss Delmege tells me she needs to close down while she spends time with her relatives in Yorkshire. It's a pity, because her cooking is very good and suits my diet and appetite. Also, she has been very attentive and always asks me how I am, which has made me feel safe and able to call on her help in the event of my becoming unwell again. However, she has given me an address in Cheyne Walk – a Miss Gillespie – so it will probably prove to be equally suitable.

Your little party does sound like a bit of a disaster. But on the whole, I think the boys' Madame has been very good to you. Perhaps I should drop her a line and thank her. It would help me to revive my French, which is now getting very rusty. I might need to try and get a dictionary; perhaps I might find one in a second-hand bookshop in King's Road.

I can hardly wait for you to see my new dress and tell me what you think of it. It's mainly fawn in colour with dabs of green, blotches of purple and splashes of red and blue running all through. Something like *The Last Rose of Summer* – do you remember that collage I started, based on the poem? A sad, subdued and plaintive thing. I'm wearing the dress now, but it should look good in the blaring sunlight of Mont Louis. I'm not sure Miss Delmege approves, though. Perhaps she thinks I'm mutton dressed as lamb.

Your Margaret

CHAPTER 15

MARGARET HAS COME to the end of her course of treatment. It has been a tiring process, not least because of the whole business of rising early, making her way to the hospital and then submitting to the electrical therapy which her doctor had recommended. Each session lasted a little longer than the previous one, and left her feeling too exhausted to tackle any other tasks that day.

It has all been worthwhile, however. As he signs her off, Doctor Grosvenor tells her he is pleased with her progress.

'As I warned you, Mrs Mackintosh, success is not guaranteed, but I think you have responded well.' He lifts the stethoscope from her chest. 'Your heartbeat sounds much stronger and I'm not detecting any of the irregularity that you suffered from before.'

Margaret buttons up her blouse. 'So, are we finished, Doctor? Can I think about resuming my normal life?'

The doctor smiles. 'Yes, of course. But take things gently. Nothing too strenuous.'

'And it will be all right for me to travel?'

A flicker of doubt crosses his face. 'Where is it you and your husband live? Somewhere in France?'

Margaret reminds him about the little town of Port-Vendres.

'Ah yes... The Mediterranean. My mother-in-law has an apartment in Nice. That can't be too far away?'

Not too far, reflects Margaret, but a whole world away.

They stand, and the doctor offers her his hand. 'So. Don't overdo it, Mrs Mackintosh. When do you plan to fly?'

For a moment she thinks he is using the word metaphorically, the way the French talk about 'escaping'. Had she bought herself a plane ticket, she wouldn't have been able to afford the treatment.

'I go three weeks on Tuesday, but I'm travelling by train.'

Now he looks concerned. 'Is someone going with you?'

'No, I'm travelling alone. My husband's still there. He will meet me in Perpignan.'

'It would be better if you could persuade someone to accompany you. Even a paid companion. Just in case.'

'But before that, I'm going up to Liverpool for a few days.'

'Is that journey absolutely necessary?'

Margaret feels as if her freedom is being curtailed. 'Well, I suppose not. I'd been thinking while I was in England I could manage a trip to see my late sister's lawyer. There are still some issues...'

'Well, if it can wait, I would postpone it if I were you. Until you're feeling one hundred per cent.'

She decides to treat herself to a taxi back to Chelsea and after settling in the rear of the cab takes the bundles of Charles's letters out of her bag. She hasn't yet had a chance to read the last two, and unfolds the first of them on her lap, smoothing out the creases.

Only nine days till I meet you at Perpignan. We both arrive there about the same time – 1.26, 1.36 pm. You from Paris and I from Port-Vendres. We have to wait till 3.20 pm for the train to Mont Louis and we arrive there at 6.39 pm. The fare from here is only 37 francs 35 centimes, second class. So that's not so bad.

I had a lovely morning and got through far more work than I expected – it was simply perfect – no wind but a lovely fresh air. But you must not expect to see very much progress when you come back. I go very slow because I have still so many problems to solve and the days of hit and miss or any such method are past – for me. However, I am doing all I can, so you must not be down-hearted or blame me if I don't produce a lot.

She puts down the letter for a moment and finds herself thinking about what Charles meant by 'hit and miss'. He used to paint quickly in his excitement to make his *idée fixe* a reality and there were times when he would scrub at the paper, trying to erase an unintended effect, and then paint over it. The forgiving nature of gouache, she thought. Watercolour is more exacting, and she's pleased that he has learned to take his time, consider where he is going, and move unerringly towards his goal. Every brush stroke will count.

You must steal Miss Olga Lindt's little pekingese – steal her too, so you can have the peke, and I can have the Olga.

Margaret laughed at this. Olga was a friend of theirs at the Blue Cockatoo. She had admired Olga's little dog, and it had crossed her mind more than once that it might be nice to own one. Trust Toshie to have designs on the dog's rather voluptuous owner.

The tailor gentleman has no corduroy trousers of the colour or length that I would like – he is going to get some more, but they may not arrive before I leave. He says this, but I don't believe him – his winter period is over and he will get no more till October or November – and I don't blame him either because all the men are wearing blue or mustard colour.

I am very excited about your new dress. Are you wearing it now, or are you only going to put it on in the blaring sunlight of Mont Louis? Never mind what Miss Gillespie thinks of it – it will do me good when I see you walking in it through the Pyrenees.

Replacing the letter in the bundle, she reminds herself that she really should get round to replying. But first, she has to go and see Meg. Dear Meg. She had a lovely evening with her and Fergus at the beginning of the month, and now she has quite got over her little stomach upset.

*　　*　　*

Although the rain is beginning to get heavy again when she leaves the boarding house, she sets out nevertheless, thinking her umbrella will keep her dry. But she underestimates the downpour, and while the umbrella keeps her head and shoulders dry, the bottom of her coat is getting very wet indeed, some of it soaking up from the puddles. Callow Street is only a few blocks away from Cheyne Walk, but by the time she reaches Meg's house, Margaret is exhausted.

Meg opens the door and lets out a little yelp of surprise as she sees her friend waiting on the step, under her umbrella.

'Margaret! How lovely to see you! Come in, come in!'

Margaret flashes the rain off her umbrella before resting it in the hall stand, and Meg helps her off with her wet coat. Then she gently takes Margaret by the arm and helps her up the stairs to the sitting room.

'Can I offer you a drink, Margaret? You look as if you could use one. How are you?'

Margaret isn't sure if she should have alcohol, but she is no longer under doctor's orders. 'Well, all right. Do you have some sherry, perhaps?'

'Yes, do you know, I believe I have.' Meg exits briefly to the kitchen and returns brandishing a dark brown bottle. 'Fergus brought this back from Spain.' She takes two small glasses out of the sideboard and pours them each a measure. As she hands one to Margaret, she asks 'Do you know this one, Oloroso? I think it has quite a subtle flavour.'

'I like the colour.' It's tawny, tending towards pink. Sitting down next to the fire, Margaret takes a sip from her glass. She finds the drink light, but warming. 'Oh, that's good, Meg. Not too sweet. No, I've never had it before.'

Meg sits on the floor at the other end of the hearth. 'And how was your hospital treatment?'

'Exhausting, frankly. I'm really very pleased that it's finished.'

Wide-eyed, Meg listens while Margaret describes the procedures which she's been subjected to for the last two weeks.

'Oh, my darling. What you've been going through! You should have had somebody with you. Why didn't you ask me?'

Margaret shrugs. 'It's one of those things. I just needed to get on with it. Get through it, you know?'

'And Charles? How's he been managing on his own?'

'He spends all his time painting. But he writes what he calls his daily chronicle, and I'm still getting a letter just about every second day.'

'Oh, my goodness!'

'I've been feeling rather guilty because I'm not quite as assiduous as he is, but I'm getting better at sending him a daily reply.'

'I'm surprised you've had the energy. You shouldn't feel bad.'

'Look. Here's today's epistle. He says he has to take the day off work tomorrow so that he can settle down and answer all the questions I asked him in my last letters.' She paraphrases. 'He says he has only two interests, me and his work, and that he finds letter writing a heavy task. You would hardly think so; I already have more than twenty long letters from him!'

'Dear Charles,' says Meg, thinking an occasional letter from Fergusson would be quite a treat.

Margaret quickly scans the letter which she hasn't yet read. 'He says he's looking forward to seeing me at Perpignan Station. All sorts of gossip and questions and answers can wait till we meet.' She looks up from the page. 'If you saw his letters, Meg, you wouldn't think he had anything left to tell me.' She passes this one to her friend, pointing to a paragraph near the bottom of the page. 'Look what he says here.'

Meg reads aloud, 'In your last letter, I hear a little cry as if you were tired of being alone. Well, Margaret, I have hated being alone all the time – nothing is the same when you are not here. Everything has a flatness – I feel as if I am waiting for something all the time, and that is true because I am waiting for you. Dear Margaret – it will not be long until we meet again.'

She drains her glass. 'That's so sweet. How lovely that he can still say that to you after you've been married all these years. I wish Fergus would write something like that to me.'

'I'm sure Fergus loves you very much.'

Meg gets up and perches on the arm of the chair opposite Margaret's. 'Yes, he does. Almost as much as I love him.'

She glances at the letter again. 'What does this mean at the bottom? "MMYT"?'

'Oh, that's just how he always signs off. It means "to My Margaret from Your Toshie".'

Meg responds with her tinkling laugh. 'You must really be looking forward to seeing him. Are you ready for the journey?'

'To be honest, no, I'm not. I'm afraid I left my sun hat in Port-Vendres. The thought of that boat crossing... If only Frances was still alive...' She suddenly finds herself in tears. 'I'm sorry...'

Coming over to the sofa, Meg puts her arm around her. 'Margaret, darling...'

'Doctor Grosvenor said I really ought to have somebody with me, but really, that's out of the question.'

'I'd gladly go with you, Margaret, if I could. But I'm afraid I have too many commitments at the moment.'

'Oh, Meg, I wouldn't have dreamed of asking you...'

'Or Fergus. He would have been happy to accompany you, but he's still in New York.'

'It's too much to ask, Meg. Even if he'd been around.'

'Nonsense, Margaret. We're friends. Is there nobody else...?'

Margaret wipes her eyes. 'Really, I need Toshie with me. I'm not a good sailor. I really need to hold on to him. Do you know what I mean?' She finds her eyes welling up again.

'Of course. I know exactly what you mean.' She reaches for the bottle and refills Margaret's glass.

'Oh, I'm not sure if I should...'

'Medicinal, Margaret.' She swivels around at the end of the sofa and tucks her legs up under her. 'Why don't you tell Charles to come and meet you at Dover? You could both stay there for a while until you feel fit to travel. There's a reasonable hotel that Fergus and I have stayed in a couple of times.'

'Oh, I can't ask him to come all that way.'

'Why not? Charles says he enjoys train journeys.'

Margaret is beginning to come round to Meg's point of view. 'Well... he has been telling me that I should let him know if I need him to come over, so I suppose...'

This is all the encouragement Meg needs. 'You've spent your life looking after Charles, Margaret. It's time he looked after you.' She gets up and goes to the bureau, returning with some notepaper, an envelope and postage stamps. 'If you write to him now, he'll get it in time.'

Margaret looks reluctant, but she can see the sense in what Meg is saying. 'All right. I'll do it when I get back to Miss Gillespie's.'

'No. Do it now, before you change your mind. Then I'll know that you've done it. We can send it by registered post from Harrod's. Tell him to bring your sun hat.' Meg moves a dining chair over to the bureau. 'Here. Make yourself comfortable. I'll just get the address of that hotel and then I'll put the kettle on.'

*   *   *

25th June 1927.

My dear Margaret.

I got your letter luckily just as I was going out to work, so I stopped and read it and got a great surprise as I had not yet picked up the registered letter that has come from Harrod's. Now the passport is my only difficulty and if I get it, I can leave here on Monday at a quarter-past two and arrive at Dover between half-past two and three o'clock on Tuesday. If I don't get the passport on Monday, I must wait till it comes, as I would have trouble both getting out of France and into England without it. Anyway, we won't be leaving Dover for Mont-Louis till Thursday so there is lots of time, but I will aim to be at Dover on Tuesday if possible.

I shall get the luggage sent on to Mont-Louis and only bring with me to Dover the bare necessities. I am in a difficulty about your sun hat, but I will find a way. I don't yet know what has happened to change your plans – perhaps the letter from Harrod's will explain this. I know the Lord Warden Hotel very well and have stayed there frequently.

I shall post this by the 2.15 train and it should reach you on Monday morning. If I manage to get the Harrod's letter in time I shall write again and post it at seven o'clock so it should reach you on Monday night or Tuesday morning. And if I have to write again, I shall post it to the Lord Warden Hotel, Dover.

Now, dear Margaret, keep quite cool. Go very slow. Don't get excited, and when I am soon with you everything will be all right.

MMYT

CHAPTER 16

THE LITTLE YELLOW train climbs back up the Cerdagne valley towards Mont-Louis. It is the last leg of their journey, and this time it seems interminable. They have brought books with them, but neither is in the mood for reading. They doze, on and off, continuing to check their progress each time the train stops at a station.

Finally, they trudge into the hotel where they are greeted warmly by the proprietor.

'*Monsieur et Madame Mackintosh. Bienvenue à l'Hôtel Jambon.*'

As they sign the register, he adds, 'I have given you the same room as before. I think you liked it.'

'That's very kind, Monsieur,' says Charles. 'As soon as you've given us the key, we're going to collapse.'

The proprietor nods with a smile that reveals he had no idea what Charles meant.

'We're going to sleep, Monsieur,' Margaret explains, placing her hands together and inclining her head on them. '*Nous avons voyagé toute la journée et nous sommes très, très fatigués.*'

'*Ah, c'est ca. Dormez bien!*'

* * *

In the morning they descend to the dining room for breakfast, feeling refreshed and ready to greet the day. Charles spots a familiar face – an old man sitting alone in a corner of the room, reading a copy of the *News of the World*. As they look around for somewhere to sit, Charles nudges Margaret's arm.

'See that man over there. He's Mr Wakefield. The one I told you about. I told him he should stay at this hotel, and he wrote to say how much he loves it.' He lowers his voice. 'I hope I don't live to regret it. He talks a lot.'

'Is he on his own?' asks Margaret.

'He travels with his daughter. I expect she's still in bed. Do you remember? I accompanied them on a couple of walks when it was too windy to paint.'

'Oh, yes. The Irishman.'

At which point they are spotted.

'Ah, Mackintosh! How the hell are you, my man? And this is your wife? You've done it again, you scoundrel, I'll have you know.' He stands as they approach his table and shakes Charles's hand before kissing Margaret on both cheeks. 'When in Rome,' he says.

'Margaret, this is Mr Wakefield,' says Charles. 'My wife, Margaret.'

Mr Wakefield gestures to them to join him at his table.

'I've done what again?' asks Charles.

Mr Wakefield laughs. 'You remember. You told me how wonderful this hotel was, and I wrote you and said that it was even more beautiful than your description, and I fully expected that the same would be true of your wife.'

Charles smiles, recalling the letter he'd received.

'And it is.'

'What?'

'True! Keep up, man! Your wife is more beautiful than you described her.'

Margaret makes a dismissive gesture. 'Toshie told me you had your sixty-first birthday in Port-Vendres. You don't look sixty-one, Mr Wakefield.'

'You're very kind, but you know I've never seen anyone so healthy looking as your husband. It must be all the fresh air and sunshine. You've chosen a wonderful place to live at Port-Vendres, so you have.' He pronounces it 'Port Venders'.

'It's a painters' paradise. Did Charles tell you we have that in common?'

Margaret nods, remembering what Toshie had said in his letter.

'And your daughter?' asks Charles. 'Is she joining you for breakfast?'

'Edith will be down at any moment.' Handing the menu card to Margaret, he glances over his shoulder. 'Ah, here she is now.'

For some reason Margaret has been expecting a young girl, but naturally she is middle-aged. After the introductions, she tells Margaret, 'Your husband was so kind to us in Port-Vendres. Both Father and I suffered from a bout of food-poisoning, although Rosa looked after me very well, didn't she, Charles? Afterwards, both Father and I felt a bit low, so Charles said that he would show us around the outskirts, and we had a wonderful circular walk, didn't we? I'm sure you must know it, Margaret. Didn't you call it the "Enchanted Valley", Charles?'

Charles nods. 'We have our own names for all our favourite places.'

'And what was the forest? The Cypress Wood?'

'Cistus,' corrects Margaret.

'Oh, that's right! The Cistus Wood. There were so many things to see, and Charles was such an excellent guide.'

'You know some interesting people, too, Charles,' says Mr Wakefield. 'The two artist fellows, what were their names?'

'Rudolph and Edgar,' says Edith.

'Ah, yes. Rudolph what? Ely? And Edgar Hereford. That's right isn't it? They invited us for a meal.'

'They had come over for dinner with me in the hotel the day before we had our walk,' Charles explained, 'and afterwards I introduced them to these two good people. So they asked us if we'd like to go over to Collioure after our walk and listen to some gramophone records.'

'We had a recital that lasted about an hour and a half,' says the daughter. 'Absolutely delightful. And afterwards their landlady made dinner for us. It was a superb meal, and – do you remember, Charles? – she apologised to you for not having entertained you so well on the previous occasion.'

'Ah well, we'd had a bit of sticky evening, although I thought I had managed to smooth the troubled waters. Margaret will tell you diplomacy isn't exactly my strong point.'

'Charles isn't the most tactful person in the world,' Margaret agrees.

Charles beams at her. 'Whereas Margaret clearly is.'

'Well, obviously, they'd all kissed and made up by the time we got there,' says Mr Wakefield.

'We had a really lovely time with Charles, Margaret,' says the daughter. 'We both began to feel as if we had known him for a long time. All our lives, really.'

* * *

Later, when they have all finished breakfast and parted company, Charles and Margaret share their impressions of the Irish father and daughter.

'I felt as if I had known them for a long time, too,' says Charles. 'A very long time.'

'Oh come, come. He's not that bad.'

'You might not be saying that by the end of the week,' he laughs. 'When you told him he didn't look his age...?'

'I was really thinking he looks much older!'

'I thought so! They're very easy to tease, aren't they?'

'But what did you make of his painting, Toshie? Did you see any of his pictures?'

Charles snorts. 'He may be a member of the Royal Society, but he paints like an amateur with no experience. He can't draw, he couldn't do anything except sit painting in the front street and the bigger the crowd, the better pleased he seemed to be. He did these miserable little watercolour pictures that your early Victorian ancestors wouldn't even have hung in the toilet, and he wasn't in the least ashamed. I find it incredible that any man should be prepared to show such drivel, or be seen doing it by any of his fellow beings.'

'But... apart from that...?'

Charles looks at his wife, who seems to be asking the question in all seriousness. Then he bursts out laughing. 'But, apart from that, he's a perfectly nice fellow who would talk the hind legs off the proverbial donkey.'

* * *

With the onset of cooler weather, Charles and Margaret return to the coast. The staff at the Hôtel du Commerce welcome them back, greeting them fondly. Rosa embraces Margaret as if she were a member of her family.

'I was so worried about you, Madame Mackintosh,' she says. 'And your husband was missing you terribly. We all felt so sorry for you both, but especially for Monsieur Mackintosh, because he was like a *bateau* without a rudder.'

Their rooms on the first floor are ready and waiting. They have hardly settled in when Kim knocks on Charles's door to tell him that his two *comrades* are downstairs in the bar.

'Charles! Good to see you back.' It's Rudolph Ihlee, still wearing his driving goggles, with his friend Hereford hovering near the door. 'We were just passing and thought we may as well call in to see if you had returned. *Et voila!* Is Margaret with you?'

Charles says she is upstairs, recovering from the journey.

'We thought you might want to come over to Collioure this evening and have a meal with us.'

'That's kind of you,' says Charles. 'But really we're both a little tired. Why don't the two of you come here and join us for dinner?'

So it is decided, and at eight o'clock the two boys return, having bathed and changed. They look suitably dressed for the occasion. Charles meets them in the dining room.

'Margaret's still very tired,' he says, 'so you're stuck with just me again. She said to tell you that we look forward to coming over to Collioure sometime soon.'

Monsieur Déjean brings a bottle of the house wine to their table and proudly announces the menu in his best English.

'We have a special dish of grilled *jambon* and tomatoes, or a very good leg of lamb and your favourite cherries for dessert.'

'*Très bien, Monsieur. Jambon pour moi, s'il vous plait,*' says Charles, and their host compliments him on his French.

As they wait for the main courses to arrive, Charles remarks that he has a little difficulty eating at times. 'I should probably have gone for the lamb. It'll be easier to chew than the ham. My tongue has swollen up again,' he says. 'I'm sure it's to do with my tobacco. Since the Americans took over the firm it's not the same, and, you know, I have to open the pack that it comes in and dry it out before I can use it. Otherwise it's too moist. Plus, with the moisture, of course, you get less tobacco for a given weight, so it costs you more. Which I suppose is why they do it – the damned scoundrels. I've been switching to *picadura* – the stuff they use for cigars – but I don't like it nearly as much as the original tobacco.'

'I ordered the lamb,' says Rudolph, 'but I'd be just as happy with the *jambon*, if you want to swap.'

'Kind of you,' says Charles. 'Perhaps I should.'

They are tucking into their meals when Rudolph suddenly declares that he'd almost forgotten to tell his friend about the horse that went for a swim in the harbour.

Charles nearly chokes on his lamb. 'The what?!'

'It was amazing. Last week there was this white horse that had come in with a dray of wine barrels, and when they let it out of the shafts it jumped into the sea from the edge of the dock. They thought they were never going to get it out.'

Edgar takes up the story. 'You know, the side of the dock is far too high, so it was never going to be able to climb out. They had to coax it over to the far side, but for a while they thought it was just going to keep swimming around until it exhausted itself and drowned.'

'There was a fearful row,' says Rudolph. 'Everybody shouting and making suggestions what to do. You know what they're like. Eventually they got it over to the shore in front of the Settlers' Bungalow. And, would you believe it, it just walked ashore as if nothing had happened. Can you imagine? A horse swimming all that distance?'

'But the amazing thing was, later on, it tried to do the same thing again. The first time just seemed to be an accident, but now it was trying to do it on purpose. As if it hadn't learned anything from its earlier experience. They ended up trying to build a wall with the barrels to keep it away from the edge.'

'Perhaps it enjoyed it,' Charles suggests.

'Nobody thought it would ever get out alive this morning,' says Edgar, 'but somehow it knew better and was willing to risk it again.'

'Maybe it was like when you're drunk,' says Rudolph. 'Just because you survived it the first time, no matter what it cost you, or nearly cost you, it doesn't stop you from doing it again.'

Charles thinks to himself, 'Well, you should know.'

'For a while after that, they kept trying to keep it away from the edge by lashing it with the whip.'

'Maybe that was what it was trying to do – to get away from the whip.'

'Maybe'

When the desserts arrive, Hereford asks, 'How did Margaret get on with the galleries?'

Charles tries to put a positive slant on it, but, with no promise of an exhibition, even the meagre prices suggested now seem optimistic.

'It looked for a while as if *Homes and Gardens* might use either my *Pinks* or *Anemones* picture for one of their covers, but Margaret couldn't get them to commit. In the end she had to go and wrest them back.'

'Why don't you exhibit in Collioure?' asks Rudolph. 'You know some of the artists there pay for their drinks at the bar with their pictures. And we have any number of tourists.'

Charles raises an eyebrow. 'Do you sell to tourists?'

'He only sells his sketches,' says Edgar. 'They wouldn't pay the prices that serious work is worth.'

'Why don't you try it?' suggests Rudolph. He fails to notice Charles's disapproving look. 'Didn't you do some nice sketches of the workmen unloading the boats at the quay? I'm sure you could find something picturesque and commercial that you could knock off in a couple of hours for a fast buck!'

'Are you an artist or a prostitute?'

Charles means it as a gentle jibe, but there is an awkward moment when nobody speaks. Edgar gives Rudolph a sideways glance before giving a slight cough and asking how Charles is getting on with his 'Rock' picture.

'It's finished! I'm quite pleased. I'll show you it after dinner.'

'When you come over, I'll show you my *Red Landscape*,' says Rudolph, and before Charles can say anything, he continues, 'and, no, I'm not going to sell it to any tourist!'

* * *

Next day, Margaret accompanies Charles as far as the tunnel, at which point she says she has come as far as her depleted stamina will allow, and she will see him back at the hotel. Charles hasn't brought his painting equipment, but he does have the little stool that Ihlee gave him, and a copy of *The Observer* under his arm. It will be a day of reconnaissance to determine what his next subject will be, and he strides out purposefully towards the lighthouse.

In the evening, the two go down to the dining room, and are welcomed at their table by Monsieur Déjean.

'It is good to see you eating with us, Madame.' Glancing around he remarks pointedly and loudly enough for the other diners to hear: 'Not all our guests choose to eat in the dining room, and Rosa has often much cleaning to do in the bedrooms.'

'*Ne vous inquiétez pas, Monsieur,*' Margaret assures him. '*Hier soir, je ne pouvais manger rien.*'

He suddenly realises that he might have been implying Margaret ate in her room last night. 'Pardon, I didn't mean...'

'*Ça ne fait rien,*' says Margaret.

'It is these scoundrels who think that they can afford to stay in a hotel, but can't afford to eat there,' says Charles.

'I do not for one moment think that you and Madame are scoundrels, Monsieur,' says Déjean, *sotto voce* this time.

As soon as their host leaves their table, Charles also lowers his voice. 'I thought I was going to be the one not eating tonight.'

'Oh? Are you unwell?'

'We had cherries last night. They were perhaps a little on the ripe side. I think I might have eaten too many.'

'Oh...' Margaret's concern changes to mild amusement.

'I was halfway along the Chemin de la Jetée when I had a sudden urgent need...'

'And did you manage to...?'

'Yes, it was a little awkward, but...'

'Your corduroys...?'

'My corduroys survived. But it was touch and go.' He drops his voice again. 'I found a stone wall and crouched down behind it. And when I was finished, I suddenly spotted a boy looking down on me from high up on the road, about five hundred yards away. It's a strange thing, isn't it? There is all this open countryside – not a soul in sight – and yet, the minute you want – need – a bit of privacy, people seem to pop out of nowhere.'

'Oh dear.'

'I'm sure he didn't see anything he'd never seen before.'

Now Margaret is having trouble keeping a straight face. 'Well, at least, you got it over with.'

'Yes, but that wasn't the end of it!'

'Perhaps you should not be eating dinner?'

'No, no. I was all right afterwards. It wasn't that.' He breaks off his story as Monsieur Déjean arrives with their dishes and serves them each with a great show of silver service. Charles continues: 'It was Ihlee's damn stool. The one he got in Paris. I found this perfect little spot to sit and read, quite near the lighthouse, looking back across the bay. I could almost see you, Margaret, sitting outside the hotel. I knew I shouldn't have bothered with the stool.'

'Why? What happened?'

'One of the nails that hold the leather on to the leg tore clean through the material and then there was nothing to stop the leg kicking out. So down I came, sprawling amongst the Cistus plants.'

Finally, the picture he conjured up makes Margaret laugh aloud. 'Did you hurt yourself?'

'Only my pride!'

'But the little boy wasn't still watching?'

'No, not the boy. But our crow was there, of course. Circling round as usual. He found it immensely funny and laughed more heartily than most human beings could.'

Now Margaret is practically helpless at the thought of the crow laughing at Toshie's distress. Charles, however, is oblivious. 'I can get it mended if I have a leather washer sewn on to the broken bit – the quality of leather looks nice and good, but you can see where it has come apart that it has a strong resemblance to superior brown paper, because it is quite a clean tear. I'm not at all convinced that my moderate weight would account for this tear if the leather had been first class.'

But Margaret is laughing too much to take in any of this Toshie-like analysis.

* * *

As Charles's tongue continues to give him problems, Margaret eventually persuades him to arrange a consultation with the local doctor. He dreads it, because he feels his French is inadequate, but Margaret is happy and willing to accompany him.

The doctor spends a long time examining Charles's mouth, and feels the tongue between the tips of his fingers. He hardly needs Margaret to explain his initial reaction.

'I do not like how this looks, Monsieur. Not at all. I think you must see a specialist.'

There is a lot more to follow, and Charles waits patiently while Margaret listens and then translates.

'He says you will have to go to Paris. They need to take a biopsy.'

Charles shakes his head. 'I'm not going to Paris.'

'*Mais, il faut que...*'

'Tell him I'll go to England,' says Charles. 'I'll see your man Randolph. He did wonders for you.'

They pay the doctor for their brief consultation, and then together they return around the harbour. Neither speaks. They are both lost in their thoughts. Finally, Charles says, 'The French have a word for it: *déjà vu*. Only this time it's me that's going to England. Your Toshie.'

Margaret puts her arm around him, and they make their way back to the Hôtel du Commerce.

CHAPTER 17

MARGARET FINDS CHARLES asleep in his clinical hospital bed, the sumptuous white pillows and blankets starkly framed by the painted tubular structure, the oxygen cylinders and the black rubber tubes. She pulls a chair up as close as she can get it to the bedside cabinet and sits there for a while, taking in his sleeping form.

At the foot of the bed stands an easel and on it one of his paintings of the harbour at Port-Vendres. They brought it back with them in Rudolph Ihlee's car, after he so graciously offered to drive them all the way from the Roussillon to London. And now the painting is there to remind Charles of the happiest time of his life.

Charles looks so peaceful that Margaret hesitates to wake him. One of his arms is on top of the covers, so she places her hand over his, and waits to see if there is any sign of him stirring.

Then he opens his eyes.

'Oh, hello.' His voice is thick, his swollen tongue making it difficult for him to form the words.

She asks, 'Did you sleep well?'

'Well enough.' He makes an effort to slide out of the covers a bit, and Margaret finds a second pillow to prop him up. 'I had a strange dream.'

'What was your dream? Tell me about it.'

'In a moment.' He looks away, unable to meet her eyes. It takes him a moment to summon up the effort and the courage to speak. 'This is probably the last time I'll be speaking to you.'

She pats his hand. 'They're going to do it today?'

He nods. 'The tongue has to go. Ah, well. But we can still communicate. Meg's teaching me sign language, but we're not getting very far. Can't do it for laughing.' He pauses to catch his breath. 'And, of course, I'll write...' He gives an ironic little chuckle, and Margaret surreptitiously brushes away a tear.

'So, what was your dream?'

'I was in a forest. I think it was that one just inland from Collioure. You remember? Where the track that goes up to the vineyard passes through the pine trees.'

'The Enchanted Valley.'

'I was walking between the tree trunks, and then they were no longer the stems of trees, but the wooden uprights in the library. The library in the School of Art.'

'Your forest.'

Charles smiles. 'My forest.'

He starts to cough, and Margaret pours a glass of water and offers it to his lips.

'There was a thick mist around the tree trunks, and then I realised it wasn't mist at all, but smoke, because the library was on fire. The books were burning. I could see the smouldering jackets of *Bannister Fletcher* and *The Seven Pillars*.' Charles grimaces with the recollection of his dream.

'And then a fireman approached me through the smoke and said, "Don't worry, Mr Mackintosh. We shall soon have the fire under control. We'll save the library for you." And for a while it looked as if the smoke was abating.'

'What would Mr Freud make of that, I wonder?'

'I wonder,' says Charles. He swallows, trying to ease the pain in his throat, and Margaret hands him the water glass again. 'After a bit, the Buildings Committee appeared. They were all there: Fra, Fleming, John Burnet – the lot of them. And they were scratching their heads and saying how they would just have to raise sufficient funds to rebuild it. Can you imagine, Margaret? They wanted to rebuild the library, all the rich dark-stained wood, just the way it was.'

He takes the glass from her and with difficulty drinks half of it, before placing it back on the bedside cabinet.

'But before any of them knew what was happening, the fire had regained hold and the whole building went up in flames. Burnt to the ground, Margaret. What do you think Mr Freud would have to say about that?'

It is Margaret's turn to smile. 'I think Mr Freud might have suggested you had an unfulfilled wish.'

'To burn the place down? No, I don't think so.'

'To outlive your own building?'

'Not even that.'

Margaret stands up and walks to the window, from where she can see the classical forms of the terraces opposite. 'We think of buildings as eternal, don't we? But, of course, they're not. How many of the great works of architecture can you think of that no longer exist? Paintings, on the other hand...'

'Paintings get destroyed as well.'

'Of course, but when they're valued, they're cherished in a way that buildings seldom are.'

'They can be wrapped up and put away. And if they're found and taken out again, then they're just as they always were. Buildings, on the other hand...'

'Buildings can fall down. Go on fire.'

'Maybe nothing lasts,' says Charles. 'Maybe we're foolish to imagine that we change the world, when the world changes despite us.'

Margaret takes his hand again. 'I think it will be a long time before that world changes.' She points to Charles's painting at the foot of his bed. 'And maybe you've already done the impossible. Frozen it in time. Made it last forever.'

The painting suddenly seems to take on another purpose. The frame has become a window through which they are looking at the landscape reflected in the sea, the landscape as they both had seen it, with forms and colours unique to the eyes of artists. The work of art is now a representation of their union that transcends the temporal nature of life, and they are not just looking at a painting: they are looking at Port-Vendres.

'You are a great architect, Mr Mackintosh,' says Margaret.

Charles manages a muffled laugh. 'You must remember, Margaret, that in all my architectural efforts, you have been half, if not three-quarters of them.'

Forcing a smile to mask her welling sadness, she continues her theme. 'But you are also a great painter. In fact, it would be no exaggeration to say, a genius of the first order.' She kisses him. And for a moment the two of them pass through that window and enjoy one last hour back at the harbour front of Port-Vendres.

Charles Rennie Mackintosh died a few months later on 10th December 1928.

There was a small funeral the next day at Golders Green Crematorium.

His ashes were scattered, according to his wishes, over the Mediterranean at Port-Vendres.

Margaret Macdonald Mackintosh returned to France, where she died on 7th January 1933.

Afterword

MUCH HAS BEEN written on the subject of Scotland's most famous architect, Charles Rennie Mackintosh. Naturally, most of this canon relates to his portfolio of work, the origin of and influences on his style and the analysis of this output. As always, behind the genius lies a man whose personal life was not straightforward, his lack of recognition leading to bouts of depression, but at the same time buoyed up by his extraordinarily supportive relationship with his wife, Margaret. That story has come to light through the remarkable series of letters which Mackintosh wrote to his wife during their separation, after they had moved to the South of France, and has been told in the form of a biography by the actor John Cairney.

My interest in retelling the story as a novel stems from my belief that this form, akin to the screenplay of a biopic, can add an expressive dimension to the story and bring it to life with a richness that cannot be conveyed simply by the rehearsal of the facts. There will be purists who will object that we cannot know the detail of conversations between the protagonists, and so much of the dialogue, and some of the scenes, will be based solely on conjecture. How then can we be expected to distinguish fact from fiction? In defence of the form, I would say that this tension exists in every drama that depicts real characters: the writer has to invent what they say and some of the contexts in which they say it, but this does not detract from the essential facts that underlie the imagined part of the story.

Whilst I have deliberately created some scenes from my imagination – those in Italy, for example, where much of what Mackintosh has to say is based on lectures given after his solo trip as a student – the key events depicted here are based on real circumstances, as evidenced in the wealth of documentary material. I have tried not to present plausible situations involving real people as if they really happened. For example, the meeting with Picasso referred to in Chapter 9 may never have taken place, although it is quite likely, as they were in the same location at the same time. Nevertheless, I resisted embellishing this likelihood with dialogue that may have served only to reinforce the notion that they did actually meet.

I hope that the reader will forgive the small departures from known facts and come to experience the emotional pull of the unique and exquisite relationship between Charles and Margaret Mackintosh.

Bibliography

Agnoletti, Fernando, 'The Hill House, Helensburgh, Erbaut von Arkiteckt Charles Rennie Mackintosh', *Deutsche Kunst und Dekoration*, 15, 1904–5, pp 337–61.

Billcliffe, Roger, *Architectural Sketches and Flower Drawings by Charles Rennie Mackintosh*, London, Academy Editions, 1977.

Brown, James, 'Mackintosh's Ayrshire Connections: Architectural and Familial', *Charles Rennie Mackintosh Society Journal*, 92, 2007, pp 11–3.

Cairney, John, *The Quest for Charles Rennie Mackintosh*, Edinburgh, Luath Press, 2004.

Crichton, Robin, *Monsieur Mackintosh: The Travels and Paintings of Charles Rennie Mackintosh in the Pyrenees*, Edinburgh, Luath Press, 2006.

Emerson, Richard, 'The Architect and the Dancer, Margaret Morris, Mackintosh and the South of France', *Charles Rennie Mackintosh Society Journal*, 98, 2014, pp 21–30.

Fiell, Charlotte, and Peter Fiell, *Mackintosh*, Cologne, Taschen, 2017.

Grol, Karen, *Mackintoshs Atem (Mackintosh's Breath)*, Lehrensteinsfeld, Stories & Friends, 2018.

Harris, Sheila, 'Charles Rennie Mackintosh at Glebe Place, Chelsea, London', 78 Derngate Archive, 2017 https://www.78derngate.org.uk/archive/charles-rennie-mackintosh-at-glebe-place-chelsea-london.

Howarth, Thomas, *Charles Rennie Mackintosh and the Modern Movement*, London, Routledge, 1977.

McKean, John, and Colin Baxter, *Charles Rennie Mackintosh: Architect, Artist, Icon*, Broxburn, Lomond Books, 2000.

McLeod, Robert, *Charles Rennie Mackintosh*, Feltham, Middlesex, Hamlyn Publishing Group, 1968.

Moffat, Alistair, and Colin Baxter, *Remembering Charles Rennie Mackintosh*, Beverly, MA, Voyageur Press, 1989.

Muthesius, Hermann, *Das Englische Haus*, trans Janet Seligman, London, Crosby Lockwood Staples, 1979.

Robertson, Pamela (ed), *The Chronycle: The letters of Charles Rennie Mackintosh to Margaret Macdonald Mackintosh 1927*, Glasgow, Hunterian Art Gallery, 2001.

Robertson, Pamela, and Philip Long, *Charles Rennie Mackintosh in France 1923–7*, Edinburgh, National Galleries of Scotland, 2005.

Robertson, Pamela, *The Mackintosh House*, Glasgow, Hunterian Art Gallery, 1998.

Storie, Roy G, 'The Geographical and Historical Significance of Dunure and Fisherton in the Setting of North Carrick, Ayrshire', 2005 https://blogs.glowscotland.org.uk/sa/public/fishertonpsandeyc/uploads/sites/8415/2016/11/roy-storie-dunure.pdf.

Stratton, Mike, 'Mackintosh in Walberswick 1914/1915', *78 Derngate Archive*, 2017 https://www.78derngate.org.uk/archive/mackintosh-in-walberswick-1914-1915.

Acknowledgements

THE ROAD FROM manuscript to published book is a rather long one and I want to thank the many people who have helped me along the way. Firstly, though they won't necessarily have been aware of their contribution, both John Cairney and Professor Pamela Robertson by virtue of their published work, provided the springboard and confirmation that there was enough available material on the Mackintoshes' private lives to make this project viable. Next, the friends who agreed to read my draft and were brave enough to comment freely, especially Lois who, without my having asked her to, returned the text fully proof-read and annotated. Three reviewers then provided me with positive and encouraging remarks: Peter Trowles, the former curator of the Glasgow School of Art, the actress Kara Wilson who played the role of Margaret Mackintosh in the 1987 *Dreams and Recollections* on Channel Four, and not least the art historian Richard Emerson whose own thoroughly researched work has been another invaluable resource.

Editors typically do hard work behind the scenes and have the thankless task of remaining invisible to the reader. So many thanks to Rachael Murray at Luath Press for the entertaining and enlightening process that we have been through together.

Luath Press Limited

committed to publishing well written books worth reading

LUATH PRESS takes its name from Robert Burns, whose little collie Luath (*Gael.*, swift or nimble) tripped up Jean Armour at a wedding and gave him the chance to speak to the woman who was to be his wife and the abiding love of his life. Burns called one of the 'Twa Dogs' Luath after Cuchullin's hunting dog in Ossian's *Fingal*.
Luath Press was established in 1981 in the heart of Burns country, and is now based a few steps up the road from Burns' first lodgings on Edinburgh's Royal Mile. Luath offers you distinctive writing with a hint of unexpected pleasures.
Most bookshops in the UK, the US, Canada, Australia, New Zealand and parts of Europe, either carry our books in stock or can order them for you. To order direct from us, please send a £sterling cheque, postal order, international money order or your credit card details (number, address of cardholder and expiry date) to us at the address below. Please add post and packing as follows: UK – £1.00 per delivery address; overseas surface mail – £2.50 per delivery address; overseas airmail – £3.50 for the first book to each delivery address, plus £1.00 for each additional book by airmail to the same address. If your order is a gift, we will happily enclose your card or message at no extra charge.

Luath Press Limited
543/2 Castlehill
The Royal Mile
Edinburgh EH1 2ND
Scotland
Telephone: +44 (0)131 225 4326 (24 hours)
email: sales@luath. co.uk
Website: www. luath.co.uk